Imperfect Paradise

Dan Dembiczak

ISBN-10: 1493742590
ISBN-13: 9781493742592
Library of Congress Control Number: 2013921231
CreateSpace Independent Publishing Platform
North Charleston, South Carolina

For my mom

"*She was flushed and felt intoxicated with the sound of her own voice and the unaccustomed taste of candor. It muddled her like wine, or like a first breath of freedom.*"
—Kate Chopin, *The Awakening*

Chapter 1

~

This is a beautiful room, I think—one that I'm sure has been filled many times over with passion and promise. I especially love this writing desk by the television— simple, stately, sophisticated. I look down at the hotel stationery and consider writing it all down instead. It would be easier, but only in the short term. Instead, I rip a sheet off and fold it twice before tucking it in the pocket of my shirt. Souvenir.

With the exception of recent events, it can honestly be said that I always do the right thing. I mail my taxes in early March. I never put tampons in the toilet. I even tip my dry cleaner. It's this history of perfect behavior that led me to this island. But now the cranks and wheels that once kept me moving in the right direction are broken. I am veering off to the roads of frightening exposure. The skin on my face is raw—the plaster dried and chiseled away.

There is a nice breeze reminding me where I still am, this place of dolphins and dreams. He'll be here soon; I know it. Just hold on a few more minutes. I think about the lotion in the bathroom. Should I go get it? Then, I could sit at this perfect vanity and moisturize to make the moment more pleasant. Pleasant. There's nothing wrong with the word, really. Who wouldn't want a pleasant cup of tea or a pleasant weekend in the mountains? Or pleasant conversation?

I want to call my sister to tell her what's going on, about my decision. This needs to be mine, though. I open the drawer of the desk, expecting to see a Bible radiating judgment. Instead, there are flyers for exciting activities like scuba diving, swimming with manta rays, zip line tours, botanical gardens, even lunch at a vanilla farm. I see the faces of beaming children and their loving parents. The cruise with the water slide and cocktails might be fun, I think. I close the drawer and wait.

Where the hell is he? He said only nine holes. Maybe the train isn't working. Yes, there is a train in our hotel. It's a theme park, actually. For the rich and responsible. It's not like I'm not used to waiting. I'd order a tray of pastries if my craving for sugar hadn't suddenly disappeared. I bet, if I do something ridiculous, he'll fly right through the door. I could change into my bikini and attempt the hula. Or I could order an adult movie. Or empty the minibar. I can see his face. His gleaming white teeth, that smart smile. I feel his stubble against my shoulder when we embrace. I taste the sweat on his neck. Suddenly, I long for the familiar. I want to be in my frayed pajamas and Berkeley sweatshirt watching *Home & Garden Television* and not talking. I want to look up and notice something new about him.

I smell pancakes coated in coconut. Breakfast is served late into the afternoon at the resort. I wonder what I'll have tomorrow for breakfast. Or the next day. What will it taste like? Will I prepare it myself? Or maybe I'll skip it entirely again.

Chapter 2

~

People kept telling me I looked radiant. Over and over again. It was nice, but I was hoping for some other adjective. Not beautiful, not pretty, not stunning. Something else. Since I couldn't put my finger on it, I'd just have to enjoy my radiance. Perhaps I was glowing from all the champagne I'd consumed. It started with mimosas over hair and makeup. Then, the bridal party decided they needed to get me a bit bubblier before the ceremony. They said it was a tradition, or something. And there I was, surrounded by the most important people in my life, with a glass of fine sparkly in my hand and a ring on my finger. It was real and I was radiant.

I reached across our table to the bottle to replenish my good spirit, but was stopped by my husband.

"None of that today. Allow me, Mrs. Chizeck."

He did just that, and then we kissed. My sister, Nancy, who sitting across from me, gave me her knowing look. She had been crying since she first saw me in my dress. Sometimes our closeness frightened me. I could feel her loving me, thinking about me, praying. As I smiled back at her, I raised my glass to lighten the moment and then said, "To having drinks poured for me all day long."

It was not the craftiest thing to say, and it might have distanced Nancy in that she wanted this day to be constantly acknowledged and revered. I just wanted to drink champagne.

"Shall we do another round?" Michael asked.

"Sure. Are you going to carry me?" What else could I get out of my husband?

"Let's hold that thought," Michael fired back, with a boyish twinkle in his eye.

As we took another tour of our lives' biggest fans, I couldn't help but feel a bit smug, seeing all my ideas and personality punctuated throughout the reception hall. I thought planning a wedding would be stressful. Had I missed something?

"There's the happy couple!" We were stopped by an old employee of mine from my nonprofit days.

"Shelly! Thanks for coming. So nice to see you." I gave her a half hug with my arm not engaged in inebriation.

"Beautiful ceremony, you guys!"

"Michael, you remember Shelly from ArtStart?"

"Of course," Michael responded immediately, as if he had been accused. It wasn't Shelly; it was ArtStart that struck a chord.

"Well, when's the honeymoon? Where are the lovebirds off to?"

"Tomorrow. We fly out tomorrow," I said, playing it down for some reason.

"Two weeks on the beautiful Big Island of Hawai`i," Michael bragged.

"That sounds marvelous. Are you gonna get Sarah in the ocean?"

"I wouldn't bet on that," Michael answered, then looked at me for a laugh.

"I was hoping for Paris, but Michael wanted the sun and golf."

"Really, just the golf."

We all laughed together, and then it felt as though—in wedding reception time—the moment had passed. The brief mention of Paris had the potential to weigh me down, and I wanted to remain on the celebratory surface. I smiled politely and gazed toward the outdoor seating area, hoping for an excuse to flee. Jackpot.

"I see my old roommate from college is out on the veranda. I think I'll go out there."

Shelly sweetly replied, "Of course. It's your day." No radiant!

Michael grabbed my arm gently and kissed my neck, as if to acknowledge the still sore spot inside of me regarding our honeymoon destination. It really was silly when I thought about it. I mean, my great problem in life was that my wonderful husband wanted to take me to a beautiful island instead of the most romantic city in the world. I had spent considerable time hating myself for letting it bother me and mar this whole experience. I squeezed Michael's hand and whispered "I love you" in his ear. We were good.

Outside the true radiance reigned, as the early autumn San Francisco sun beamed down, warming us from the inside out. My old college roommate, Wendy—it wasn't a lie—was leaning against the railing that separated her from the Bay. She wore a bright yellow dress, a striking contrast to her jet black hair and gorgeous blue eyes. Adorned with bohemian jewels, hair waving about, Wendy was the picture of city girl independence. I had always admired her, and wished we had stayed closer after graduation. While I went straight into the work force, Wendy took a year to travel Asia before returning to get her master's in art history. She now ran two galleries in town, owns a flat in North Beach and regularly contributed to major art publications.

"Wendy!" I unclasped myself from Michael and sped up to give her a proper hug. She turned to me and opened up her arms, ready for me to cling to her and her exciting life.

"You wear white very well. If I didn't know any better..." Her witty response was refreshing.

"You are killing in this yellow dress! I'm so glad you could make it."

"Well, the location is perfect. And how could I miss it? I've missed you."

"Me, too. Has it really been since that Christmas party for art history alums two years ago?"

Michael inserted himself, tempering the lovefest. "That sounds about right. I recall getting poisoned by a crab cake."

Wendy laughed, genuinely. "Michael, how have you been? Still owning Silicon Valley?"

"More or less."

"Sounds like my love life." Wendy threw Michael's smug confidence back at him.

"How is your dating life?" I asked, hoping to hear that she had settled down for some reason.

"Oh, you know. I'm very happy. No one worth reporting on, really."

I expected a drop in enthusiasm, a hesitation, or lament. She was so matter-of-fact, unflappable about admitting she had no one special in her life. My breathing changed and my champagne started to take on a different taste: earthier, slightly licorice. It wasn't just that I had no response; I felt like I couldn't speak. My throat tightened. I looked at Michael for support, and he swiftly intervened.

"Well, I'm sure you're breaking hearts at record speed. The right guy is out there, if he can handle you," Michael said, awkwardly and with little conviction.

Wendy looked at both of us, confused and seemingly annoyed. I took the last sip of my champagne, only to have it go down the wrong pipe. I began coughing, convulsing, a pathetic display of bridal bad behavior. I recovered quickly enough, but it was too late. Wendy looked at me, through me, and saw fiction. She excused herself and graciously conveyed her kindest hopes for our future. As I watched her drift away, I returned to thinking about Paris and felt a strange longing to be there with Wendy. But when I looked back at Michael and ran my fingers through his slick hair, I saw images of Wendy and Paris floating above me like a pair of birthday balloons. They became smaller and smaller, until eventually they just disappeared.

Picking out our first song was a long, sometimes contentious and arduous process. Michael came up with a list of his favorite ten love songs. I hated eight of them. My list contained fifteen, to cast a wider net, but the yield was only one song we mutually loved. Michael leaned heavily toward older tunes: Dolly Parton's "I Will Always Love You," the Carpenters' "We've Only Just Begun," Elvis's "Can't Help Falling in Love with You," and every love song ever written by U2. Meanwhile, my choices drew from a more contemporary pot: Cat Power, Death Cab, Interpol, Pavement, and Magnetic Fields. The song I deemed perfect was "All We Have is Now" by the Flaming Lips, a beautiful and harrowing poem that I still view as romantic. In fact, I had to defend all my choices as "romantic" to many of our wedding's stakeholders.

Not wanting to deal with confrontation, we let the song issue slip under the rug for several weeks. Michael continued to check in on the other arrangements, and I asked for his opinion on seating charts, readings, appetizers, even linens. One Friday evening, we were sitting in one of our favorite neighborhood restaurants, a slightly dilapidated but venerable institution serving the best tapas in the Bay Area. There have been few moments in my life that felt like a painting: every exact detail pauses, and then turns into something timeless and truthful to be studied and contemplated in earnest. Sitting at a small, iron-rod two-top table in the corner of the restaurant, against a tattered saffron-colored wall, we each had a glass of red wine with a bowl of mixed olives between us. Michael was wearing my favorite suit: gray and white pinstripes with a deep purple tie. My emerald green dress shimmered in the soft light. We were right there, together, eating olives and drinking in each other. The music was faint in the restaurant so it wasn't always noticeable when there was a track shift. When we did notice, we both looked around as if we could surmise more of the lyrics with our eyes. I stopped looking around, stared at Michael's wine glass and nodded my head. We had our song, and I felt for the first time in months that my life could be art.

"From the very first moment/that's when I knew..." David Gray's caring voice filled the reception hall with sentiment as Michael and I displayed our lack of timing and awkwardness. Still, the song resonated, and I wanted to be back in that painting. I wanted olives instead of grilled salmon and wedding cake. I wanted better lighting.

"She's all yours, Pop." It was now time for Michael to relinquish me to my father, a tradition I found both creepy and sweet. My father, Mr. Arnold P. Williams, didn't look a day over forty-five, with his tux that fit like a glove and silver hair shorn off to give him that military confidence. We danced, and he told me how thrilled he was to have Michael as a son-in-law and that I would always be his girl. The part about him breaking Michael into pieces if he ever hurt me was just understood.

If there was ever a man to fear, it would be Arnold. He survived being born to a mother on her death-bed, survived years of poverty and transience, Vietnam, law school, and raising two daughters. He hated that I studied art history and made his concern for my late-blooming love life heard, loudly, in every conversation I had with him since I turned twenty-five. Now, at my ripe old age of thirty-two, we were dancing on my wedding day. His concern, while at times condescending and even hurtful, was really just the Arnold Williams way. He didn't want me to be alone, to miss out on the life he had created for us. I knew that all along, and now I got to look at him and be wistful of those times he chided me for being too "modern" or too "cavalier" about my future. I would miss those talks. Was I, to him, now "cured"?

The song ended; applause surrounded us. My father kissed me on the cheek and went toward my mother. I remained on the dance floor all by myself. The DJ was changing tracks. Silence. I looked down and noticed a tiny patch of the floor was covered in dust so thick I could write my name in it with my finger. Not everything was perfect, and it seemed just fine.

Shortly after our engagement, I began immersing myself in the oddly intriguing world of cake television. I would gobble up any cake competition, cake reality show, even people just talking about cakes. Of the many wedding details ahead of me, I knew immediately that choosing the cake would be dearest to my heart. Perhaps because, for many years, my main coping mechanism shifted between devouring a pint of dark chocolate ice cream and a package of Double Stuf Oreos. I knew cake better than dresses, appetizers, favors, wedding parties, readings, or rings.

It's not surprising then that I went through five different bakeries before finding *the one*. I made appointments with each of them, sampled their most "in demand" as well as some "emerging favorites." Michael didn't join me, trusting my good judgment in all things saccharine. He preferred chocolate, but that was the extent of his input. The first four bakeries would have all been solid choices, but something was a tad awry in, at least, one element—icing too sweet, cake too dry, too much vanilla, not enough vanilla. Whenever I mentioned that we were probably going to honeymoon in Hawai'i, the bakers would shove cloyingly sweet tropical flavors at me, like something called *lilikoi* or guava or coconut. The fifth shop was a quaint cake shop on Russian Hill, tucked away behind a row of apartment buildings. You would never notice it as a pedestrian. You had to enter through an alley, and the signage was minimal—a sandwich board outside the door placed at an odd angle. But in the increasingly catty world of cake, any bride knew of Magda's. Named after the owner and baker, the place was a San Francisco legend when it came to the perfect wedding cake.

In her seventies with a thick Polish accent, Magda ran the shop six days a week for ten hours each day. Her daughters, Rita and Nora, were her only staff. They created beautiful, ornamental cakes in just three flavors: vanilla, chocolate-cream, and vanilla-raspberry. They only covered them in fondant.

On my first visit, I rang the bell at the front desk and peered back through a pass-through to the kitchen. I heard women's voices speaking in both English and Polish. There was a faint sound of television static coming from the kitchen. Rita, the younger of the two daughters, came to greet me. She was covered in flour, sweating, and not smiling.

"You Sarah?" She got right to the point.

"Yes. I talked to your mother on the phone about..." I did not have time to answer.

"Yep, we know. Stay there. We'll get the samples." She cut me off and fled back to the kitchen.

Moments later, Rita returned with three plates. She quickly ran through the flavors and then stood over me, as if she just wanted to get the whole ordeal over with so she could return to watching TV with her family. I tried the vanilla first, which had a very slight hint of cardamom. A wave of warmth shot through me. The chocolate-cream was next, deep in flavor and rich in texture. The cream didn't overwhelm my mouth, but just hung out there a bit to help the chocolate work its way through my system. Finally, I tried the vanilla-raspberry, though in my mind I had written it off as too fruity. Plus, I really felt a strong propensity toward chocolate for both my own addiction and it being Michael's only requirement. The cake had all the wonders of the original vanilla with a burst of tartness and almost a touch of black pepper. I had expected piped in raspberry freezer jam, but this was so much more complex. I asked Rita about it, and she mumbled something about her mother's kolaches.

I stared at all three, torn, as I knew the quality of the cakes at Magda's were the highest I had tasted—and likely, would ever taste. The decision was mine, one that seemed at the moment to be the most imperative of my life.

"Which one you like?" Rita barked at me.

I thought of Michael, and what he would think if I chose a cake with fruit in it. Would he be disappointed? It was his money paying for most all of this, and I did feel like I was just running with all the decisions. I loved the raspberry cake; it was a delicious bite that I still think about regularly. I wanted to take a whole cake of it home with me that day and eat it while flipping through magazines. I fell in love with it. I looked up at Rita, cleared my throat, and gave her my order.

"This is fantastic. Nice work, babe," Michael cooed as he shoved cake at my mouth. His face was a mess of chocolate cream. I choked a little, not prepared for what it's like to be force-fed as an adult. The cake was very good.

With the dance and cake behind us, my feet and back were telling me to find a seat somewhere. I grabbed an entire bottle of champagne and made a beeline toward our family table, joining my sister and mother. My mom was reapplying her makeup, having been a teary-eyed mess most of the day. Meanwhile, my sister was tidying up the table, despite there being an array of overpaid help nearby. Typical Nancy behavior. She always volunteered to clear the table, do the dishes. She would come over to my house sometimes and just start cleaning. I opened the bottle of champagne and watched her, wondering where that motivation came from and if I would soon inherit it. Would I have three kids and make bologna sandwiches? Would my walls of fine art be replaced by crayon drawings of owls and happy people on Ferris wheels?

My mother spoke first, saying, "You must be exhausted."

"Just my feet. How are you holding up?"

"It's getting close to my bedtime, but I don't want to miss a minute."

"Thanks, Mom. Really."

"Of course. I admire your calmness. I don't think I've ever seen a bride so even-keeled. Have you, Nancy?"

My sister awoke from her trance of stacking plates. She looked up, as if she hadn't noticed me before. "I don't think so. Sarah, I'm just so happy for you two."

Throughout the season of celebrations, that last "two" always threw me off a bit. It wasn't enough to linger for days, or even hours, but more of a fleeting nausea—like taking a vitamin on an empty stomach.

I already knew Nancy's answer, but asked anyway. "More champagne?"

"Oh, none for me. Thanks. Scotty has a soccer game at nine tomorrow," Nancy said, before going back to cleaning the reception table. I wondered if she would then get up and start on the rest.

"You know, we have hired help to do that," I blurted out, accelerated by my hundredth glass of champagne.

"I know. But it makes me happy. Gives me something to do with my hands," she responded politely, as though she were an ex-chain-smoker who just found God.

"How about you, Mom? More champagne?"

"Oh, maybe a little." Jessica Williams did not like to turn down a drink, an invitation, food, anything. It was how she was built, and I appreciated it.

"So, tomorrow, you'll be in your bathing suit drinking a mai tai..." My mother giggled as she said this, as if there was something naughty about being on vacation.

"Yes, early flight. But I figure I'll sleep on the plane."

"Text me a picture of the hotel as soon as you get there. The kids will love to see it." Nancy was now engaged simultaneously with cleaning and conversation.

"I should have plenty of time for texting. Michael plans to golf every single day."

"Are you going to join him?" My mother asked, a bit concerned.

"I doubt it. They have a spa, and I'll find things to do during the day. We'll have the evenings."

"Evenings are more romantic, Sarah," Nancy whispered, again with the weird naughty tone.

I poured myself and my mother more to drink and then sunk back into my chair. For the first time all day, I felt relaxed and not on stage. There I was with the two most important women in my life, just being themselves. My older sister was cleaning and worrying about her kids, while my mother was going with the flow—literally. The DJ had put on "Twist and Shout," and several kids were jumping up and down on the dance floor. Some of their teen siblings joined them, and soon older and older generations would follow. All the bodies soon became a riotous clump. If the song kept going, increasingly toward crescendo, I imagined everyone exploding at some point into a cloud of glittery smoke. Lucky for them, the song ended on cue. The clump separated; laughter lingered.

Our night ended not with confetti, but with heartfelt embraces, best regards, and some jealous jabs about our two weeks of glory in the sun. The car was not decorated with tin cans and shaving cream. It was a subdued silver SUV; its driver wore a black suit and had perfect teeth. As he packed away the last of our gifts, I collapsed into the back seat, for the first time feeling the impending hangover. Michael swept in beside me, and I immediately put my head in his lap. He ran his fingers through my hair, and, for the first time, I felt his wedding ring scrape against my scalp.

"You feeling okay?" he asked, in almost a whisper, as the driver started the ignition.

"Too much to drink. That's all. I'll be fine."

"We'll get you some water and Tylenol when we get home." He grabbed my hand as he said this and raised it to his mouth. I felt loved.

"It's nice to finally be alone. It's kind of hard to process the day, isn't it?" I rolled onto my back, so I could see his face.

"I was thinking the exact same thing. I can't wait to be with you—and just you—for two whole weeks."

The car smelled like new plastic and cinnamon. I put my ring finger against Michael's, so I could see the symbols together. I thought about the chaste brides of the past or the present, who had to deal with losing their virginity on top of all the other neurotic energy involved in a wedding. Of course, after four years together and a vat of champagne in one evening, I highly doubted there'd be any fireworks. I wondered if some couples, like us, chose to abstain for several months before the wedding to mimic that glory of the wedding night.

"Michael, will you help me remember my sunscreens? I bought special ones yesterday, and they're on the table in the entryway. I didn't have time to add them to our suitcases yet."

"Sure thing," he said with a noticeable quiver in his voice. He began to tear up a bit, not something you'd see very often in Michael Chizeck, Stanford MBA and business animal.

I touched his face, feeling a bit of scruff coming in near his jaw line. He grabbed my hand, as if to regain control of his masculinity.

"God, I love you," he said.

"I love you. You okay?"

"I'm fantastic. Just so happy." Even Michael Chizeck was susceptible to tears of joy.

The moment could have continued its dreamlike quality, but I didn't want Michael's vulnerability to get the best of him. Or maybe I wanted him to save up, so I could see this side of him more often.

"What did you think of the food?"

"Everything was wonderful. You did a fantastic job. Your mom seemed to enjoy those shrimp."

"Indeed," I laughed, "and did you see Nancy trying to clean up?"

"Classic Nancy."

As we continued to download the ceremony and reception, my stomach calmed down, and I felt refreshed by the normalcy of the conversation. Whether it was commenting on so-and-so's outfit or how

13

so-and-so looked amazing after surgery or hearing of someone's remodeled kitchen, I felt like my favorite blanket had been placed over me.

By the time we reached our driveway, I was already dreaming. I was in a church, a large cathedral. At the altar was my father, dressed in a hazmat suit. I was in my wedding dress, but the floor began to flood with sea water. My father started to speak, but I couldn't hear him over the sounds of rushing water and an organist somewhere behind me. As the water engulfed me, I could see my old roommate, Wendy, emerge alongside my father in the same brilliant yellow dress she'd worn to the wedding. She reached out her hands to me, and I tried to swim toward the altar, but the current was too strong, and I went under. Then, I woke up, in a cold sweat.

"We're home, sweetie. Were you having a bad dream?"

I looked up, and there was my husband. No drowning.

"I was drowning."

"Another one of those? I thought they would stop once the wedding was over."

"Probably just residual stress," I responded vaguely.

"Come on. Let's go inside."

The driver unpacked our gifts and placed them on the dining room table. Michael grabbed my sunscreens from the entryway, and we walked upstairs for our first night as husband and wife.

I was one year older by the time I got my gown off and hung up in its museum-like casing. Feeling unencumbered, I took my time washing the pounds of makeup off my face. I wanted every surface cleansed of decoration. There were a few stubborn spots, which drove me to furious scrubbing. Michael came into our bathroom and saw me looking as though I'd just had acid splashed on my face and put his arms around my waist. He looked at me through the mirror, making me self-conscious.

"Hey, I'm washing my face," I said with a subtle laugh.

"I see that. Are you taking off a layer of skin?"

"I just don't want to look like a hooker on the plane tomorrow," I said, then realized I was in my bra and underwear.

"Okay. I'm going to bed. Be there soon?" Michael was already down to a T-shirt and boxer shorts, his usual sleeping attire.

"Yep. Almost done." I turned and kissed him passionately, for some reason.

Michael kissed me back, almost forcefully, luring me with a trailer version of what he had to offer later.

"See you soon then." Michael smiled and went to bed in the other room.

I watched him walk off, and then turned back to the sink. My face still wasn't as clean as I had hoped, but I turned my attention to putting clothes on. Our master bathroom was adjacent to our closet, a feature I immediately fell in love with when we first saw the house. I could spend hours in the bathroom and closet areas, taking baths, rearranging my shoes, staring into the mirror, looking for something.

Instinctually, I went for my favorite pajama bottoms. As I started to step into them, though, I considered something sexier. I had a few negligees collecting dust, including a surprising shower gift. I dug one out of an underwear drawer and held it up to me in front of a full-length mirror. I kind of liked my body. All the Pilates, hours on the elliptical machine, and dieting for my special day had me tighter, firmer, and more erect. I peeled off my underwear and unclasped my bra, letting it flop to the floor. My breasts stared back at me as the final two congratulations of the evening. I stood there, admiring myself, for several minutes before covering up with my slinky sex uniform. The silk excited my flesh. The closet, the house, all seemed somewhere else.

As I sauntered into the bedroom, I heard Michael already snoring. I laughed to myself, still feeling turned on, perhaps all for myself.

Chapter 3

Having lived on the West Coast my entire life, it was probably odd that my first trip to the Hawaiian Islands was happening in my thirties. It's not like there hadn't been opportunities: Michael traveled to Honolulu a few times a year for business; a group of friends from high school went for their senior trip while I stayed back to take art classes in Carmel; when it came time for our first major vacation as a couple, Michael suggested Maui, but I talked him into Spain instead. It's not like I'm averse to the tropics. I like palm trees and indiscriminately fruity cocktails. I just hate the ocean. I mean, being close to it. Irrational fear, I suppose. I swim in pools occasionally, but even that isn't something I treasure.

The hangover was cured by our gracious flight attendant, who brought me a Bloody Mary minutes after we boarded. In my twenties, I always thought of first class as something to aspire to, a dream of some type, or the once-in-a-lifetime splurge. It's funny how, over time, these things become the norm, and we come to expect them. Since Michael's career really took off three years ago, I have not been in coach once. I wonder, though, what it would feel like if I had earned it.

After my third Bloody Mary, I finally felt normal. I began reading the in-flight magazine, *Hana Hou*, to find out what shenanigans I could get into once we landed in Kona. Or Kailua. I don't know. It's very confusing. Is it Kailua-Kona? To my left, Michael was all coffee and ambition, reading the paper and squinting. I flipped through the magazine, blazing past advertisements featuring adorable families in luxurious condos, proudly wearing smiles and hibiscus-print. I couldn't imagine living on a tropical island. What would I do all day? I settled on an article about spear fishing—a woman who became renowned in the male-dominated world of it. While I had no aspiration to kill fish or be in the water, I immersed myself in this woman's story. Doing this was her purpose, her passion. It's not like she was a lawyer during the week, and then hopped on a catamaran on Sunday after some mojitos and knifed a few. She lived for the art of it. I finished the article, closed the magazine and then my eyes. I thought there might be turbulence, but Michael assured me there was none. The rocky sensation would be due to dehydration. I felt ready for a checkout.

I awoke to a petite woman with flowers in her hair placing a large platter in front of me. Michael had taken the liberty to order my meal for me while I was in a deep sleep, enjoying another recurring nightmare of not having enough credits to graduate. Before me was a mix of fruits, cheeses, and a croissant. My hot entrée was bananas foster French toast while Michael had selected the croquet madame. I was sweet, and he was savory this morning, apparently. The flight attendant asked if I wanted anything to drink besides water, and I responded negatively in such a way that took my body the least amount of effort. I felt like I had just woken from anesthesia.

"I hope you like it. Bananas foster French toast." Michael pointed to it proudly.

"And I see you have my favorite." I reached over and tore off a piece of his sandwich.

"A little bit of France after all," he joked and began forking his fruit deliberately.

I picked at my French toast, enjoying it but underwhelmed. I really wasn't all that hungry. I took a piece of pineapple, then a strawberry, then a cube of Gruyère. I looked over at Michael again. He was now sinking his teeth into the eggy, bready goodness. I could have been annoyed that he had ordered for me, that he had mentioned France again, and that he was eating with his mouth slightly open. But as I took another bite of the toast, I closed my eyes and let the explosion of rum and sugars come over me. Michael wanted me to have this experience, something new. Just like this trip. He loved me. I took another healthy heaping of my sweet treat and fed it to him, a morning-after reenactment of the cake feeding from the night before.

We ate the rest of our meals in silence before our friend with the flowers came and snatched the plates away, asking again if we needed anything. I was ready for caffeine. She returned with a cup and saucer of piping hot Kona coffee. She was very proud of the Kona part, mentioning it three times before beaming a smile and an "aloha" at me. She was young and perky, probably mid-twenties. I wondered if she was married, but, by the time I thought to look for a ring, she had been whisked away to assist other passengers.

"How much longer until we land?" I asked Michael, as I reclined my seat and gazed out the window.

"About two and a half hours until Honolulu," he responded immediately, not needing to check his watch.

"Oh, that's right. I keep forgetting there's a layover. How long is it again?"

"About two hours. Enough time for a couple mai tais." He grinned and grabbed my knee.

The overhead announcement came on about the in-flight movie. It was a romantic comedy I had no interest in. I, instead, opted for the small digiplayer with a number of movies, old TV shows, and documentaries on it, so I could control my entertainment. Or maybe I would just go back to sleep.

Michael opted for neither. Instead, he flipped through the same in-flight magazine I had encountered earlier.

"No movies, huh?" I asked, watching him excitedly flip through pages of resorts and golf course advertisements and cookie coupons.

"Nah, too excited. I may read my golf magazines in a bit. Did you bring anything to read?"

I realized I had not packed a single bit of reading material. Now that there was no longer a need to bury my face in bridal magazines, I was at a loss.

"No, I guess I'll have to buy something when we get there."

He flipped through to the same page I had glared at earlier, of the family blasting cheer amid the backdrop of their tropical vacation home. His reaction was much different, though.

"Wouldn't this be great? I wonder if I could talk people into letting me work remotely in the winter."

I looked out the window, searching for the appropriate reply for a wife of less than twenty-four hours.

"One can dream." I said, sounding like an idiot motivational speaker.

We spent the remainder of the flight mostly in our own worlds. I watched a documentary on whales, a random episode of *Weeds*, and the beginning of a Harry Potter movie—all the while letting my mind wander into other spaces. I changed from coffee to white wine at some point, and finally got a look at the flight attendant's ring finger—and name tag. Her name was Polly, and she was single, or, at least, portraying herself as such. She gave a generous pour of pinot grigio for my second round, and I thanked her. My instinct was to tip, but that would be weird and probably not allowed. Instead, I thought I'd make small talk while Michael lost track of time with his putters and holes.

"Thanks, Polly. How do you like working here?"

"You're very welcome, ma'am. I love this job. It's, like, the best one I've ever had."

"That's nice. Have you had a lot of different jobs?" I started to feel awkward, not knowing how to relate to this ball of youthful positivity in front of me.

"Oh, you know. I was a surf bum for a while, and then I went to community college and then lots of restaurant work. I live on Oahu, and I'm just always trying to get outside as much as I can."

"Oh, that makes sense. Well, it was nice meeting you."

"You, too. Enjoy your stay on the islands. Anything else I can get you right now?"

A new personality, I thought. I used to be able to communicate with ease, but, over time, I had lost so much of my ability to spark a conversation with a stranger. I became very adept at the customer/help relationship. That I could do very well. This is what happens when one stops working, I guess.

"No, thanks," I said, forcing a smile.

As our plane made its final descent into Honolulu, I took in the deep blues and bright greens. I saw a surprising number of skyscrapers and highways, lit up in golden hues that glistened rather than imposed.

"We made it," Michael cheered, as he put his magazines back into his carry-on.

I followed him to the front of the plane, where we were greeted with alohas and *mahalos*. They seemed to love to say "thank you" on this airline. The open-air airport was both impressive and confusing. The air was thick, bold, and enrapturing. I began to sweat, enjoying the fragrances as we trotted along to check on our connecting flight.

My first trip to Disneyland was in second grade. My parents had surprised us for spring break. We took the car and drove down the coast to Orange County, arriving at the magical spot on a scorching afternoon. Our car's air conditioning only moderately worked, so we were all sweaty and uncomfortable. Nancy asked if we could go to the hotel to cool off in the pool before going to the park. I agreed with her, wanting to enjoy the Magic Kingdom feeling my absolute best. Having an older sister made me think of these things, rather than forge ahead like a sloppy eight-year-old. She was thirteen and embodied a whole world of sophistication to me. My father was very upset. He couldn't fathom our request, deeming us "spoiled" and "disrespectful." The diatribe continued for several minutes, citing "less fortunate" children, financial burden, and "careful planning."

My mother looked back at our faces stained with tears of shame and whispered, "It'll be okay." And it turned out to be fine, as we forgot about our discomfort once we got on the log ride and cooled off with the speed and splashes.

We reached a screen, and Michael noted that our flight was on time. We had two hours to kill. He asked me what I wanted to do, and then began walking toward one of the tropical-themed airport bars. I followed him, feeling sticky and rushed, remembering my mother's voice. It'll be okay.

We sat at a two seat table with a tropical fish tank to our right. In it were brightly colored fish, some coral, and a tunnel made out of rocks, presumably for the fish to play in. I opened my menu and went straight for the drink list. Each cocktail had some thematic name, like Painkiller or Tropical Itch. Michael informed me that these were actually standard tropical drinks, not specific to this bar. I almost ordered a martini, but Michael convinced me to get into the spirit with a mai tai.

"Extra shot of rum for seven dollars?" the super-excited server asked me and then smiled as though she were waiting to be crowned the winner on a game show.

"Definitely for me," Michael responded and then looked to me for agreement.

"Hell, it's our honeymoon." I smiled as hard as I could back at the server.

"Any food for you? Kalua pig nachos? Spam sliders?"

I thought she was joking, but, after laughing and then watching her face drop, I looked away at the fish.

"Not right now. Maybe we'll keep a menu in case." Michael smoothly slid a menu to the left corner of the table, employing his usual powerful people skills.

Outside of the bar area was the main restaurant, oozing with excited kids about to see turtles and wear shells for the first time. I noticed one boy, probably nine years old, flipping through a book of tropical fish and saying each name out loud.

"Dad," he screeched, "I bet we'll see this one at Molokini."

I wondered, If I had spent time in the ocean at that age, would I have overcome this silly phobia?

"They are headed to Maui," Michael informed me. "That's where Molokini is. From what I've researched, Kohala is a much better spot."

Our gigantic mai tais appeared before us, complete with an umbrella, cherry, and pineapple wedge in each—the universal emblem of the tropical honeymoon. Michael raised his glass to make a toast.

"To Hawai'i. To Us. To the next two weeks being about nothing but us."

He could always pull stuff like that out of a hat while I found myself constantly fumbling to not only say the right thing, but avoid the offensive.

"To us." I clinked his glass and then took a huge sip.

Sweet would be a heavy understatement, but, after five sips, I didn't care. It reminded me of the juice of my childhood: sugar and corn syrup with a touch of something citrus. My body warmed, my pulse increased, and my eyes widened. I was thankful for that extra shot. I was thankful for that moment, sitting in a theme restaurant bar with my husband, not having to worry about children or wedding vendors or walking down the aisle. My only agenda item was to be at the gate on time for our fifty-two minute flight to Kona. I planned to drink as many of those juices as possible. I wanted to keep drinking until I had enough courage to jump into the tank with the fish, gliding through the toy tunnel with the grace of the fish I admired.

"That's us, Sarah. Come on. We need to board."

I looked up at Michael as he held out his hand. I felt like I had been wrapped in some type of adhesive and pressed into the bench at the terminal. He looked funny, not like deformed or anything, just sort of generally ridiculous.

"Come on. We'll get you some water on the plane."

I tried to stand with the grace of an arthritic war veteran and leaned into Michael for support. I had been drinking a lot more than usual in the last few weeks leading up to the wedding, between the dinners, events, and just general anxiety over getting everything perfect. Yet, somehow, I had misjudged my tolerance. Those damn extra rum shots. People around us began to stare, empathy for the mess of a woman about to board first class with her rich husband. I looked at Michael as we showed our boarding passes and started to laugh. At first, it came out as a small hack, but, by the time we walked through the jetway, I was in hysterics.

"Come on, Sarah. Let's get you to your seat."

"Look, Michael. We're in a tunnel. Like the fish. We should swim." I was hammered.

"Oh, boy. I need to watch you and the mai tais." Michael tried to laugh it off, but he was not able to fully disguise his frustration.

He got me into my seat, again next to the window, and then sat down himself with a heavy sigh.

"Are you mad?" I asked, then laughed in his face.

"Of course not. It's just...how did you get so wasted?" He was now laughing himself.

"I love Hawai`i," I said and leaned in to kiss him, but missed and hit my chin against the seat.

"I love you, drunk lady."

"I think I'll go back to sleep now. Wake me up if there are stories."

"I'll do that." He leaned his hand over and moved my hair away from my face.

I closed my eyes and gave into the spinning. I imagined myself back in that fish tank, an inebriated mermaid governing her plot of sea. I couldn't feel my nose.

After twenty minutes, I was wide awake and pert, as if my liver had never endured my rum diary moment. I took a sip of water, straightened myself in my seat, and looked out the window. Nothing but water. Endless blue. I shifted away, looked over at Michael, and spotted a piece of wax in his ear. Finding his imperfections always made me feel better, but I rarely pointed them out. It gave him this vulnerable, feminine side that I liked to enjoy all by myself.

I reached under my seat, touched my purse and then dug for my compact. Time to assess the damage. Abused wife? Homeless junkie? Reality sensation? I was pleasantly surprised by the lack of disaster before me. After some judicious reapplying, I put my purse away and let out a great sigh. I was ready to give this my best.

The Kona Airport was open-air and quaint. It reminded me of the Burbank Airport as we descended actual steps that were hooked up to the plane, instead of a jetway. Workers scooted about, but at a much slower pace than SFO or LAX. Our first stop was baggage claim—to collect our luggage and Michael's precious golf clubs. Using the hotel's equipment would be demoralizing to him, emasculating even. All around us, people were being greeted with leis, a special welcome to the island. The greetings must have been arranged by one of the parties as a surprise, or perhaps a family member. What looked like a newly-wed couple beamed as they were "lei'd" together on the steps above us while we watched black suitcases move along the silver strip. I looked at Michael, hoping he had been watching them as well. His focus was laser-like on the baggage wheel. His attention quashed any thoughts that maybe he had arranged a lei greeting for us, at least, at the airport. I wondered what a fresh lei would smell like, as my only experience had been with the cheap, plastic things that hosts would make you wear at silly tropical-themed cocktail parties. They smelled like new car and tobacco.

After grabbing our luggage, it was a short shuttle ride to our rental car shop. The couple with the fresh leis were on our shuttle, providing what might have been the best air freshener I ever experienced: clean, floral, earthy, and bold but not overwhelming. Now, I knew. Much better than plastic. They were younger than we were, probably in their late twenties. I suspected they hadn't been together long, as they still had that starry-eyed lover thing going on. Every time I looked up, I would see one of them look at the other one and sort of laugh—with hilarious happiness.

"Where are you staying?" I asked, wanting to know more about the happy couple.

"The Royal Kona," the young woman replied, somewhat sheepishly.

"Oh, that sounds nice," I responded, not knowing a thing about the place.

"That's right in town, isn't it?" Michael joined in with his local Big Island knowledge.

"Yes, it is. We couldn't quite afford the Kohala Coast," the husband explained, though his response seemed less of a lament than a statement.

"I can't wait. I think it will be beautiful. I've been looking on the Internet, and there are so many shops and things that we can walk to... it's like we really won't even need a car!" The wife squeezed the husband's hand, and then they did the smile and laugh thing again.

"Really?" I asked, as it was unknown to me that there were any urban centers on the island. Michael had planned the whole trip. I had only seen our hotel on-line.

"Oh, yeah. We have a view of the ocean, too. And is it tomorrow we go to our first lu`au?" The wife looked at her husband, hardly able to contain her excitement.

"Yep, that's tomorrow. And then there's a submarine ride you can take just off the Kailua Pier, and, if we get really daring, there's a night dive with manta rays," the husband giddily announced.

That sounded like a nightmare, but I smiled in support. Their simplicity was contagious. I sort of wished we were staying in a motel somewhere close to them, and could spend time in flea markets. But then I looked over at Michael and remembered what we had, and that you can't go back to youth just to feel less encumbered.

"I'm Sarah, by the way. This is my husband, Michael."

"I'm Rachelle; this is David. Are you on your honeymoon as well?"

Wasn't it obvious?

"Yes, we are. In fact, we just got married yesterday in San Francisco. That's where we're from. How about you guys?" I quickly responded, reinforcing the freshness of our vows.

"Portland. We were married in Portland about a month ago. We couldn't get the time off work until now," Rachelle said slowly, a polar opposite of my defensive spew.

The four of us remained silent for the rest of the trip, periodically making eye contact and smiling while trying to look out the windows instead. The driver insisted on grabbing our luggage for us while we waited on the sidewalk. A cool breeze sifted through me, a sudden contrast to my warm shell.

Rachelle and her husband tipped the driver, took their bags, and headed toward the front entrance of the car rental storefront. On their way, Rachelle gave a fizzy wave along with a "Nice meeting you. Have fun! Aloha!"

"Cute," Michael remarked once they were out of earshot.

"Do you have cash?" I asked, already thinking past the cute couple to more pragmatic affairs.

Michael dug into his wallet and effortlessly flipped through several bills of various values. He had his aviator sunglasses on, my own cute cliché of Silicon ambition. He tipped the driver, and we trailed behind our new best friends, ending up right behind the lovebirds in line. They were rubbing noses and laughing again. Rachelle caught a glimpse of us, and then turned to excitedly greet us as if it was our ten year reunion.

"Hi! We have a coupon for a convertible!"

"Neat." I couldn't think of a better word.

"What kind of car are you guys getting?" David asked, as he grabbed Rachelle by the waist, intensifying his grip on her.

Michael and I looked at each other for the answer, quizzically asking the other without words. Finally, Michael put a stop to the major suspension.

"I think I just signed us up for the economy. Figured we wouldn't be leaving the resort much."

"Oh, that makes sense," David said sweetly, not wanting us to feel underprivileged.

"We've just never been in a convertible before," Rachelle justified, unable to hide her enthusiasm.

"That sounds like fun," I responded without thought. Though after I said it, I realized the truth of it. Riding around in a convertible on an island actually sounded fun.

"Michael, maybe we can see about upgrading. Riding along the coast with my hair whipping around sounds romantic." I leaned in to kiss him, proving to everyone we were in fact newlyweds.

Michael paused, seizing the opportunity as the line began to move and the lovely couple made their way to a checkout agent. He took his time, pulling out his phone to check the time, carefully putting it back in his pocket, opening up his wallet again to recount the bills, more carefully this time. Finally, the tasks ceased, and he answered me.

"No."

It clearly wasn't about money, or an aversion to adventure. This was Michael being practical, something he liked to imbue from time to time. His patriarchal torch flamed up, asserting his role as man of the household and decision-maker. The torch had no predictable patterns, and never really made sense to our situation. Randomly, a dessert course was denied or a home improvement project halted. He didn't need to explain, he just exuded the most powerful "no" he could muster from a deep well of masculine conviction. I could argue with him on many topics and held a significant amount of autonomy in our relationship. Perhaps, this is why I let him exercise this bit of authority every so often, as I sensed that somehow he needed it.

"That's fine," I demurred and stepped forward, as it was our turn at the counter.

People had told me our hotel was magical, that it would transcend our wildest expectations. I did not really have any of those wild expectations, except for clean sheets and good bar service. In fact, we had checked into an amusement park of luxury. As we wheeled our luggage through the lobby, we were greeted by a hotel associate who handed us each a chilled bottle of water and relieved us of the strenuous task of carting our own belongings. In between exotic bouquets and mammoth art pieces, we had arrived to a point of our entitlement I had not quite imagined. I kept losing my train of thought, my attention darting around from object of beauty to object of more beauty. The silent car ride over started to fade away as I became fixated on our new surroundings.

"Wow. This is really beautiful," I said gently.

"I knew you'd love it." Then, he kissed me.

We slowly ambled our way to the reservation desk. I let Michael do all the talking, as he made sure we had the suite he requested and double-checked all the golf course hours. Soon, we'd be alone in our room together. I wanted to just stay in the lobby and let the sensory overload cast its spell a little bit longer. For a moment, I imagined I was a little girl who had been taken away from her family. This is how I'd have to cope. Not bad, if a bit lonely. There were plenty of distractions, and maybe that was the ticket to feeling rescued.

The luxury of our suite rivaled that of the lobby and surrounding grounds. After stepping onto marble floors, I barely had time to notice the ocean view staring at me from the back of the main living room. Glass doors opened onto a private veranda. The living area featured a dark leather sofa and matching chairs (how did it survive the tropics?), a glass coffee table with perfectly fanned out magazines, a tray of mints, and a beautiful bouquet. Each side table was adorned with something equally impressive. One had a welcome basket filled with macadamia nuts, juices, bottled water, soaps, chocolates, and fresh fruit. Another had guide books, brochures on local attractions, spa menus, and the largest in-suite dining menu I had ever seen. I picked it up, only to test its girth, and smiled in astonishment. Michael and I had been to some pretty amazing hotels, but this room presented a new standard in luxury—one that made me feel equally amazed and embarrassed.

Double doors led into the bedroom, which continued along the same ocean-view wall and also had access to the veranda. The king-sized bed was as plush as expected, covered in orchid heads spelling out "Aloha." I thought about the dedication that went into the preparation, overwhelmed at the thought of messing with all the perfection. The right nightstand was topped with another beautiful floral arrangement; the left topped with something better: a bottle of Veuve Clicquot over ice and two flutes. I turned to Michael, who was behind me throughout the tour and asked, "Did you set all of this up?"

"Some of it. A lot of it was just part of the package," he said modestly, as if to downplay the romantic elements.

"It's...amazing," I said, unable to come up with a more interesting adjective.

I wandered into the bathroom after passing by a striking vanity at the foot of the bed. I imagined staring at myself with the waves crashing to my right. The bathroom was larger than my first apartment, with a

Jacuzzi tub fit for a small family, a river rock walk-in shower, the same marble floors that greeted us, and a double-sink vanity stocked with spa products. I wanted to call someone, but who was the right person?

"Happy honeymoon." Michael grabbed my waist from behind and kissed my neck. I felt safe and lucky.

"Where do we begin?" I turned around, suddenly amorous and suggestive. Michael kissed me, passionately but briefly.

"Well, for starters, we should fill the drawers up. We're gonna be here for a while."

He was referring to a chest of drawers just outside the bathroom, the one piece of furniture I had somehow ignored.

"Right. Or we could wait on that," I continued.

Michael broke things up after a few more kisses, leaving me alone in the bathroom. He returned moments later with our luggage and placed it on the foot of the bed.

"Champagne?" he asked, somehow both seductively and matter-of-factly. He could really be confusing sometimes. I watched him leave again, staring at his ass. I kicked off my shoes and turned to look at myself in the mirror. I wondered if anyone would ever call me radiant again. After hearing the cork pop in the other room, I unbuttoned my blouse, ready to give the husband a peek. I walked into the bedroom to see him pouring the glasses. I reached over to grab his ass. He did not like it.

"Hey, I'm trying to pour some expensive champagne here." he said, startled at first but then ending with a playful smirk.

We clinked glasses and took sips. I wanted him to ravage me, not in a romantic way. Rather, this was something primal. The thick air, the long flight, and the lavish surroundings had me aroused in a way that had escaped me for several years. I took off my blouse and began to unclasp my bra, letting my sinful sisters spill in front of Michael in hopes of being devoured. I didn't even care about being kissed. Michael took another sip—a big one—and then set his glass down. He moved toward me, burying his face in my breasts. I set my glass down as well, grabbing the back of his neck and letting out a slight moan. I reached down to pull his shirt off, wanting to run my fingers through his chest hair and feel his muscles. Just as I started to pull up his polo shirt, he backed away from me. He walked past me, past the bed. I stood there, topless, my back to my husband who had just rejected me and stared at the ice beginning to melt in the champagne bucket. The taste on my lips soured. I slumped down on the side of the bed, defeated and embarrassed. I poured myself another glass, chugged it and then began to put my bra back on.

"I'm sorry," Michael said from behind.

"Just surprised. That's all," I responded, body frustrated.

"You just seemed...different."

"And that's a bad thing? We're supposed to keep it interesting, right?"

"Well, yeah. I'm sorry. I just felt out of my element for a bit. I'll make it up to you tonight. After dinner."

So now we had appointment sex? I let out a huge, passive-aggressive sigh as I pulled my blouse back on.

"Sarah, talk to me. Are we okay?" Michael was now sitting on the other end of the bed.

"Fine," I almost whispered, not wanting to turn around.

"Hey, I'm gonna head out and play some holes."

Did he realize what he just said? I remained silent, hoping it would squelch my desirous thoughts.

"So, why don't you settle in and check out the hotel? Maybe find a restaurant for dinner?"

Not wanting for this blip to define our honeymoon, I pulled myself together as I mentally drenched myself in ice water.

"It's fine, Michael. Have fun. I know how excited you are to have this time away from work." I stood up and turned around as I said it, smiling down at him.

"I love you. And I am serious about tonight." He got up on his knees and kissed me. I liked being the one standing.

I watched him walk away, this time not objectifying him but merely staring at his form. When I heard the door shut, I collapsed on the bed again and immediately touched myself. Closing my eyes, I let my imagination take me to new heights. I came harder than I had in several years.

I dizzily stumbled to the shower to atone for my moment of ecstasy, leaving a trail of orchid heads that had stuck to me. It's not like I didn't masturbate on a regular basis; this was different. This was deliberately disconnected from Michael, and more powerful than even the best sex between us. Or with anyone. Letting the warm water pulsate on my back, I unwrapped a bar of papaya-ginger soap and smelled it. I gently washed my entire body, hoping to get every crevice purified. When my flesh started to journey back to the land of arousal, I reached down and turned the cold water up to halt any potential rediscovery.

Dried off and poised to be less of a sexual tornado, I wrapped myself in one of the plush white robes hanging on the back of the bathroom door. I looked wistfully at the other one, for a moment imagining Michael and me—sitting side by side, eating scrambled eggs and reading the morning paper. But then I opened the door and let the robe and the thoughts disappear, as I focused my attention on the dresser I had ignored at first glance. I did not like the idea of settling in for two weeks, but digging into a suitcase every morning for my underwear seemed equally undesirable. I reluctantly dragged my luggage across the room, hastily unzipped it and sloppily threw clothes into the drawers. I hung a few things in the closet and emptied the entire contents of my toiletry bag into one drawer. That's as much as I could commit to living in a honeymoon suite.

Dressed in a white summer dress, cut just above the knee, I felt appropriate for my place in this moment. I held my breath as the elevator descended to the lobby floor. What should I do? When the door opened, a crowd of children charged at me. Their parents were behind them, seemingly not paying attention. I skirted around, gasping for breath, unusually startled. I looked around, realizing I had nowhere to go. My sense of direction skewed, I paced around in a circle before spotting the concierge desk in my periphery.

Behind the desk stood a man, a boy really, smiling at me with perfect lips.

"Aloha," his smile said.

"Aloha there," I returned, still not feeling right about how I said the word.

"Can I help you with something? Answer any questions?"

"Um. I'm not sure."

"Did you just check in?"

"Yes. I'm here on my honeymoon."

"Where's the lucky guy?" he asked, all the while holding that perfect smile.

"Playing golf. I'm supposed to find us a restaurant for dinner tonight."

"Of course. Do you wish to dine at the resort or somewhere along the coast?"

"Oh, I guess somewhere here. At least, for tonight."

"Absolutely. My name is Kalei, by the way."

The name struck me, as there was nothing ethnic about this boy. He was probably somewhere near twenty-six, dark wavy hair left a bit shaggy without being sloppy, dark almonds for eyes, skin that probably tanned well. But definitely a white guy taking on a Hawaiian name.

"Hi, I'm Sarah." I reached out my hand, something I don't always do when dealing with customer service situations. He reached out and connected his flesh to mine, disrupting my train of thought.

"Pleasure to meet you, Sarah."

Time paused, and we exchanged friendly eye contact. Letting go of his hand, I felt an inexplicable wave of embarrassment. Was I attracted to this kid? I did not deny myself the enjoyment of eye candy, but my attention had never drifted toward younger men. Uncomfortable with the idea of leading a predatory fantasy life, I changed my tone.

"So, Kalei, what would you recommend for dinner?"

"Well, Sarah, what are you hungry for?"

Why did he have to say my name again? And was he being flirtatious, or was I just on the cusp of becoming a raging sex addict?

"Oh, you know, seafood and the local flavor."

"Well, I cannot give you authentic local flavor here. But I can suggest some excellent dining. Hale Nani would be a nice place to ease into your vacation. It's in the north tower, near the fountain. The chef is fantastic."

I wondered what he meant about the local flavor, but hesitated at engaging more. My eyes darted from his lips to his name tag as I made a mental note of how to spell his name, and then across his chest. Just as I felt that electricity from earlier start to work its way back into my system, I cleared my throat and extended my most purposeful hand.

"Thank you very much for your help. Aloha."

"Aloha, Sarah. Enjoy your stay and feel free to stop by the desk anytime."

I turned around and began walking toward the elevator as it was the only path that I could easily follow. I went straight back to my room and took another shower.

"Aloha," I mumbled into the phone with a mouthful of Bavarian cream.

"Sarah!" Nancy screeched back.

"We made it."

"What are you doing? How's the hotel? How's married life?" She had so many questions, it was debilitating.

"I'm sitting on the sofa in our room in a robe eating a plate of desserts from room service."

"That's what you're eating? Where's Michael?"

"He's playing golf, of course. I got a recommendation from the concierge for dinner. A kid named Kalei." Why was I mentioning his name?

"Scotty won his soccer game!" she blurted out, as though her son were the only person on the team.

"That's great. Give him a hug from Aunt Sarah. Have you ever had passion fruit donuts? They are amazing. And coconut cream puffs, and a rum-pineapple crepe. I'm going to weigh two hundred pounds by the time I leave!"

"Sounds like you're having a nice time. How's the weather?"

I looked down and realized I had cleared my plate of desserts. I yearned for more and considered hanging up and placing another order.

"It's sunny, I guess. I haven't really been outside, but it's clear, and there's a nice breeze."

"Oh! We should talk about the brunch. Do you just want immediate family?"

Nancy was referring to a brunch she wanted to host for us when we returned. We would open all of our gifts in front of people over pancakes and bacon. It sounded weird, but it seemed really important to her and many people told me it was a tradition.

"Let's keep it small, yeah."

"Well, how about the Sunday after you get back?"

I looked down at the empty plate again, not wanting to commit to another wedding event or think about any kind of schedule.

"Let's wait until I get back. I'm trying not to worry about the calendar for the next two weeks." I tried to let this drop as elegantly as possible.

There was a moment of hesitation before Nancy responded. I imagined her trying not to have an aneurysm.

"Okay. Let's just not wait too long. People get very busy in the fall, you know?"

"Sure. Sounds good. I should probably get ready for dinner."

"So romantic! Watch the sunset for me. I'll be making the boys turkey burgers. Exciting, huh?"

I decided not to respond.

"Take care. I'll text you some pictures tomorrow and call you in a few days."

"Take your time. Aloha!"

"Aloha."

After hanging up, I looked down again at the perfect landscape of crumbs and bits of cream. I thought of dinner later at Hale Nani, the resort attire requirement, and Michael eating something with chop sticks. I curled up a bit on the couch, letting part of my robe ride up a bit, so my bare flesh could stick to the cool leather. I knew another tray of desserts and a bottle of wine would ruin my appetite, but I embraced the sudden streak of indolence and dialed in my order for another assortment of island confections and a bottle of Sauvignon Blanc. Minutes later, the cart was rolled right in front of me. I tipped generously, not a bit ashamed of my gluttony.

About an hour later, Michael found me asleep on the couch, clutching a stemless wine glass with a few drops still in it. He woke me gently, removing the glass from my hand and moving the tray of desserts off the couch and onto the coffee table. My robe was agape, my parts displayed in squished and awkward positions. He sat down at the foot of the couch and kicked off his shoes.

"I guess dinner will have to wait for tomorrow," he said as he poured himself what remained of the white wine into the glass he unhooked from my hand.

"Sorry," I said, half meaning it and half just wanting to go back to sleep.

"Just as well. We'll enjoy it more tomorrow. We'll have the travel washed off and have a good night of Hawaiian sleep," he said, and then chugged the wine as though it was last call for seats at the opera.

"You should order something. It's really good." I glanced down at my second plate of devoured desserts.

"I see. Sweets?" he asked in a subtly judgmental tone.

"Guilty," I declared, and then extended my foot to his lap for a rub. Something ought to come of this honeymoon!

"I may order a burger or something in a bit. Sorry I was late. The course is phenomenal. Met this gorgeous, older couple from Atlanta. You would just love them. I told them we'd have to have drinks one night. Recently retired, I think."

He continued to chatter away about the game, how his clubs fared in the tropics, the brilliant couple from Atlanta who lived frugally for ten years, so they could retire early and spend more time together. I just let him talk as, the more lost he got, the more he would keep digging his knuckles into the sole of my foot. I closed my eyes and thought of the moment I spent with myself earlier, after he left me for golf. He didn't know what he missed.

I switched feet as he segued into a tirade on the expense of college education. He then switched back to golf, and the Atlanta couple who apparently had two children who both went to state schools. I decided I'd be comfortable sleeping on the couch for the night, and let myself drift back to where I'd been before, and smiled.

People warned me that I wouldn't be able to sleep late in Hawai'i, and, at seven o'clock in the morning, I was wide awake—perhaps even perky. I sat up on the couch with the equivalent of a spring in my step. In my butt? I looked out toward the sea, hearing the waves crash lightly, a round orange sun on the cusp of beginning its daily roast of red-headed tourists without proper sunblock. I looked over at the bedroom door, which was shut. Michael must have stayed up reading after I drifted off. I got up, the bathrobe loosely draped over me, and wandered out to the veranda. It seemed not a single person was up yet; I had the entire resort, the ocean, the subversive sun, all to myself. I leaned against the ledge, breathing in the serenity amid hints of chlorine and what I later came to identify as plumeria. Today would be my, our, first full day on the island. I paced back and forth on the veranda, not nervously, more of a contemplative glide. In the early light, the island seemed to hold a quiet vastness that I had not anticipated. There was more to this place. I thought again of Kalei's remark about the genuine local flavor. I thought of his face, his hands, and then tried to divert my imagination back to passion fruit donuts. My senses were erupting just as the golden ball of paradise began to creep her way up from her slumber.

"Up early?" Michael spoke in a gentle tone, but still startled me.

I quickly turned around to see him there, in just his boxer shorts with his hair messy. I liked how he looked in the morning—another reminder of his vulnerability.

"I was all slept out, I guess," I responded as I walked toward him and gave him a good morning peck. He hugged me, and, as we held each other, the placid state of moments just before turned to a golden hue of morning stir.

"So, I thought we could shower up and check out the breakfast buffet," Michael said as we came apart.

"Oh, sure. Sounds great." I felt like I had just eaten, but a sunrise buffet sounded nice.

I thought of suggesting showering together, something we had never been very good at enjoying. The last time we did was out of sheer convenience, as our hot water tank was about to die. The time before that, we were both drunk and sweaty from an afternoon wedding reception. We awkwardly attempted to please each other, but ended up laughing more than anything at our clumsiness.

"I'll let you go first. I'll go see if the morning paper is at our door and order up some coffee," Michael beamed, seeming to vanish immediately.

The buffet was as epicurean as Michael described it, with a Nutella fountain, full bar, sushi, omelet stations, and every kind of breakfast meat known around the globe. After heaping our plates, we seated ourselves at an outside table overlooking the pool.

"Decadent, huh?" Michael remarked, as we sat down to indulge.

"At sixty-two dollars per person, it better be." I was still amazed by the opulence of this place.

I dug into a piece of smoked salmon, took a sip of coffee, and looked out at the pool in hopes of seeing people begin to undress. It was still too early. We were, in fact, the very first people in line for breakfast.

"So, what's on the agenda for today?" Michael asked, shoving a piece of Portuguese sausage into his mouth.

"I thought I'd check out the pool. Start working on my tan."

"You still don't have anything to read." Michael said this as if it were mandatory I be reading throughout vacation.

"I'll check out the gift shop after breakfast. I'm sure they have some mindless trash to keep me occupied."

"Which bathing suit are you going to wear?" Michael winked.

"The orange bikini, of course."

We continued our indulgent meal together, outside in the pleasant air, as other tourists began to make their way to the pool and buffet. The sleep in their eyes was hardly detectable, as optimism shot out like a laser aimed directly at the next point of pleasure. I wanted my orange bikini to be the last words between us for the morning. I liked the idea of Michael visualizing me as some sort of beach goddess.

"All done?" Michael asked, looking down at my empty plate.

"It would seem so. I guess I was hungry."

"We got our money's worth then. I think I'll head back to the room."

"I'll see you back there before you head out to play golf?"

"Probably. If not, we can text and come up with dinner plans. A redo from last night?"

"Yes. I promise not to drink a bottle of wine on the couch."

Walking back through the restaurant, I noticed several people in line, faces aglow and bodies relaxed. I grabbed Michael's hand, wishing to advertise our own glowing nature. There was a pond filled with bright orange koi, much like the color of my bikini that marked our juncture. Michael gave me a kiss, put on his sunglasses, and trotted off toward the room. In the opposite direction, I ambled my way toward the gift shop, in pursuit of unchallenging reading material.

I stood before the racks of magazines showcasing beautiful women alive and well amid gloomy headlines of global meltdowns. I naturally went toward the wedding section out of habit, then diverted toward pop culture. Out of the corner of my eye, I noticed a few art publications. I felt a magnetic pull toward them, but, at the same time, wanted to look away. I thought about Wendy, wondering if she had written for these magazines. What was really new in the art world? Who lived there? I was about to pick one up, my fingers extending, just maybe a peek.

"Are you going to buy that or what?" His voice was familiar, confident.

I turned around to see Kalei, from the concierge desk, standing there holding a bottle of water and a tin of breath mints.

"What are you doing here?" I blurted out, as I pulled my hand away from the allure and anxiety of art.

"Ready to start my shift. I work here, remember?" He smiled, disarmingly, and took a few steps closer.

"Of course. I guess even employees use the gift shop," I said, with a fake laugh I had never used before.

"They don't even give us a discount. Can you believe it? I have to talk to people all day long. They could, at least, provide me with some free mints." His tone was light, as nothing seemed to truly bother him. I wanted to know more about him.

"What time do you start today?"

"Fifteen minutes. I see you're looking at some reading material here."

"Well, sort of. I thought I'd go out to the pool and flip through something."

"Are you an artist?"

A small bullet shot through my abdomen. Had anyone ever asked me this before? I was the one who worked with artists, championed them. But one of them?

I returned to the fake laugh. "Oh, no."

"I just saw you looking at that magazine, that's all."

"Yeah, I'm not really sure what I want."

Kalei moved closer, asserting himself in front of the magazines. He picked one up, *Cosmopolitan*, and read one of the captions out loud: "Look ten years younger in five minutes."

I laughed, not fake this time. I snatched the magazine out of his hand.

"Sold!" I said it without thinking and felt my face heat up.

"Well, then, you're ready to start your day." He smiled and moved away toward the cashier. I followed behind him, hoping for a few more minutes of conversation.

We remarked on the weather and made other benign observations about the gift shop. He paid in cash and didn't ask for a bag. He tucked the mints in his pocket and opened the bottle of water immediately, taking a vigorous sip. I looked away, trying to concentrate on my own transaction. I paid with plastic and didn't think to decline the plastic bag.

"Aloha, Sarah," he said, waving as he walked away.

I wanted to chase after him, to continue the fun banter that had my face burning and pulse elevated.

"Aloha." I waved, deliberately not using his name.

Instead of going back to the room, I went straight to the pool. I just sat there, staring at the water, clutching the plastic bag against my chest. If this moment were a painting, where would I be? I thought about this, trying to position myself in the foreground overlooking the splash of spontaneous glee. In the background would be a couple, looking back, clouds rolling in behind them.

I spent two hours sitting there, not reading beauty tips or sipping cocktails, but framing, concentrating, and wondering which side of the pool belonged to me.

By the time I got back to the room, Michael had already left for the golf course. I had the room to myself once more, alone in luxury. Opening one of the drawers of my temporary dresser, I spotted the orange bikini crumpled up against underwear and socks. I pulled the top out, examining it almost scientifically, and then let it drop to the floor. I climbed into bed, not wanting to think about what to do next.

"This is just lovely," Michael remarked on the restaurant as he sat down, a compliment to me for finding out about it from Kalei.

It was, in fact, a beautiful setting, with tiki torches, a waterfall, pond, and enough foliage in the outdoor seating area to create privacy at every table. I had texted Michael to meet me there, wanting an excuse to walk by the front desk in my little blue dress. Kalei was not there, which I found to be equally a relief and a disappointment.

"How was golf today?"

"Outstanding. God, Sarah, I really love this place. How was the pool?"

"Very nice," I whispered, not wanting him to know the truth of how I spent the entire day.

"Looks like you were careful with the sunscreen. You must have taken a long time at the gift shop."

"Um. Oh, yeah. I decided to walk around a bit, see more of the resort. Sorry I missed you."

Michael had no concern on his face as he opened his menu with a grin, eager to digest more of this playground he loved.

"They're supposed to have good seafood," I said with unintended disaffection.

The server, a Bohemian young woman with what looked like jewelry in her hair, came by and took our drink orders. I went for the non-tropical martini I had been craving while Michael opted for a local beer. We smiled politely at each other as she vanished.

"Hungry?" Michael asked, which seemed open-ended at the time.

"A little bit. I'm thinking of a salad."

I had made sure the dessert cart had been removed from the room before I left, hiding the evidence of my despicable honeymoon ennui. Or was it? I was indulging, after all.

"Any word from work?" I quickly changed the subject, getting Michael's focus away from paradise.

"Texts galore, but I keep ignoring most of them," Michael returned, completely in control.

Michael was one of those wonders of the business and technology world, unflappable and always in command. Just six months after the ink on his MBA dried, he was running a complete division at Apple. From there, the promotions and accolades continued until he was swooped up by the bourgeoning Angel Investment Firm as its COO. He managed people effortlessly, made decisions everyone respected, and had an uncanny ability to foresee the future. At the ripe age of thirty-two—the exact same age as me—he had the perks of being able to ignore communication from all levels without the slightest fear of his job security.

Our server returned with our drinks and a basket of warm bread. The martini was dry, salty, and satisfying. Michael boasted that the beer was one of the best he'd ever had, going on about investing in the brewery. By my third martini, my appetite came back enough for me to finish my crab salad and peck at a piece of bread. Michael devoured his plate of surf and turf, leaving just a small pool of butter that reminded me of oil dripping out from under a car.

"Dessert?" Michael asked.

"No. Why?" I responded defensively.

"I just thought you might like to share something."

"Sorry, I was thinking about something else. No, I'm full tonight. Go ahead, though."

"I think I'll save my dessert for later." He smiled, reminding me of our postponed sex date.

I looked at him, wanting to use him like I had tried the day before, to get to that place I reached by myself.

"Sounds good." I smiled back at him, finishing off the last of my martini.

That night, Michael and I made love for the first time on the Big Island. I held back, resisting the urge to be slutty and primal. I gave Michael what he wanted, and we connected as we had before. Comfortable and relieved to not be alone in the room, I curled up next to Michael and made my mind go blank.

Chapter 4

～

I remembered that coffee date with Nancy last November as if it were yesterday. I can still see her face and feel the tremble inside before I blurted it out.

"So, I think tonight's the night."

I just let it hang there, like a wet towel slung over a metal rod on a windless afternoon. Its sogginess began to creep into the air, choking me. Finally, the silence summoned someone to speak.

"Oh, Sarah!"

Proud and teary-eyed, Nancy looked at me as if I'd just won a gold medal. She stopped swirling her green tea bag, picking it up and gently setting it on her saucer. I watched the green liquid ooze out slowly, infecting the perfect white surroundings of the tea cup. She then scooted her chair back, stood up, and walked around our small café table. In the middle of a busy coffee shop, Nancy leaned down and firmly kissed my head. Right there, amid steaming milk, I was being branded.

The kiss was followed by a hug, though I remained seated. I awkwardly tried to reciprocate, but Nancy's left arm began to choke me. Her perfume smelled like apricots soaked in citrus soda. I looked down at my cappuccino, wanting to take a sip before it lost its heat. I reached for it, a subtle hint for Nancy to let go and return to her seat.

"Sorry, sis. Just so excited for you." She took the clue and walked backward to her seat, taking a gulp of tea.

"Well, it's not a sure thing. But I found a ring. And he made it clear that tonight was special." I realized it was definitely happening as I said this out loud.

"It only took him, what, four years?" Nancy said in a way that walked the line between snide and jovial.

It was scarf season in the Bay Area. The balmy October had recently vanished, giving way to the brisk November air. Nancy's was coral with black-checkered print, contrasting nicely with her warm face. Mine was a simple black, one of my trusted accessories. As I looked around, though, I noticed no one else had a black scarf. All were draped in colors and patterns, some sort of extension of the faces they wore to the public.

"Oh, have we decided on Thanksgiving?" I decidedly changed the subject.

"I was planning to host, as usual. Are Michael's parents going to be in town?" Nancy said in her best business tone. I knew she wanted to get back to the engagement and my impending wedding.

"No, they won't be flying in this year. Let me know what I can bring."

"Are you thinking a summer wedding?" Nancy could not contain herself.

I took the last sip of my cappuccino—the milk cool and the espresso bitter from sitting too long. I thought about the question for a second as I tried to get the taste out of my mouth. The truth was, I had never been one of those girls who had her dream wedding planned out. I knew Michael and I were headed in this direction. It was part of the reason I agreed to stop working almost two years ago. We had just bought our place. I had reached a point of slight frustration in my career path. And we simply didn't need the money. I figured, when the time came, I could plan the wedding. Now that the moment was arriving, I felt unprepared, like a student being handed a pop quiz in first period.

"I'm not really sure, yet. It will depend on Michael's travel schedule. One thing is for sure, and that's my maid of honor." I reached across the table and squeezed Nancy's hand, pumping life and energy into her.

"Oh, I'm going to cry again." Nancy tried to laugh off her emotions.

"It's okay, Nancy. I know you'll be here to help me through this stuff. You're the expert," I assured her, and then let go of her hand to let her wipe her eyes.

"Fall might be nice. The city is beautiful in September," she said, regaining composure.

There we were, two sisters having coffee and tea in the middle of a work day, discussing the best time for a wedding. I wondered how I would spend the rest of the afternoon, before getting engaged to Michael that evening. I knew Nancy had to get back to the East Bay and her kids before traffic became too much of an obstacle. I looked around, again admiring the flair draped around the customers' necks. I eyed a younger woman wearing a scarf with bright blue and orange streaks. She had on a long gray sweater, old jeans, and a pair of boots. None of it truly matched, and yet she made perfect sense. I couldn't keep my eyes off of her. She had a to-go cup in one hand and a weekly arts guide in the other. I watched her pour a splash of soy milk into her cup—an Americano I guessed by the double-cupping. I watched her wander out into the excitement of another day in the vibrant city, and made a decision.

"Well, I guess I should head back. This was really nice. I'm so happy for you, Sarah. Should we walk out together?" Nancy was already standing up as she spoke.

I remained firmly seated and replied, "No, I think I'll linger a bit. Maybe get another cappuccino and see what's going on downtown. Maybe check out one of the new exhibits."

Nancy looked confused but not appalled. This would be one of those times when she would say something like "Oh, you're so lucky you don't have kids" and not truly mean it.

"Good for you" was her response this time, a nod to my privileged lifestyle of idle time.

We hugged, and I promised to call her first thing in the morning to give her the official good news. After she left, I walked over to the door and picked up the same weekly arts guide the young woman I admired had been holding. I opened it up, ready to embark on possibly the last pre-wedding adventure I would have all to myself.

When Michael escorted me into the Italian restaurant in North Beach where we had had our first date, the storyline I had written in my head continued. We were seated at the same table, and Michael ordered the same bottle of red table wine we had first drunk together. As our basket of warm bread was set down between us, I started to wonder where he would hide the ring. In the dessert? In the bread? Would he get down on one knee? Rather than a moment of romantic spontaneity, it started to induce panic in me. I felt like a lab rat, being watched until I found the cheese: how many minutes will it take her? What is her pulse rate upon finding ring?

"Michael, I know what tonight is about. The answer is yes."

I needed it not to be a surprise—for me, for us, for the other patrons watching me. It was an agreement to the future, one that both of us knew was coming. I felt a relief to just acknowledge that, and my appetite was conveniently coming back while the bread was still warm.

Michael looked at me, quizzically—then blankly—and simply responded, "Okay."

Our moment of choked silence was saved by our server and wine. I couldn't get my lips around that glass fast enough, anything to avoid eye contact with my fiancé.

"Have you two decided, or do you need a little bit longer?"

Michael and I looked at each other, then at our server, and then at our menus. Our astute server simply said to take our time and disappeared. Michael took a big sip of his wine, his lips turning burgundy. I followed, letting the velvety red slide down my throat like a local anesthetic.

"Was it the manicotti I ordered the first time?" I forced a lilt in my voice, searching for a moment to recapture the intended romance of the evening.

"No, it was the eggplant parm," Michael responded, without looking away from his menu.

"I'll have that then." I continued my peppy turn and snapped my menu shut.

"Do you remember what I had that night?" Michael looked at me, sharp and accusing.

"Baked spaghetti and meatballs," I replied with confidence. This I remembered.

"I'm impressed," he said with a flippant tone, then methodically closed his menu and shoved it aside. We now had nothing but the bread and wine between us, not enough to keep the elephant sized ring in the room from shining through.

I poured us both more wine, hoping Michael would make the next move. Take out the ring. Say something. But he didn't. Instead, even worse, he changed the subject altogether.

"So, how was coffee with your sister?"

"Great. She's doing well."

"What did you do the rest of the day?"

"Just ran errands and then came home," I lied for a reason that I was not completely in touch with myself.

I had spent the afternoon in the art museum, admiring new exhibits and soaking in the old greats. I left feeling inspired, renewed, and sad. It had been the best two hours I'd spent by myself, or really with anyone, in my recent past. And then there was the conversation I had in the museum café with the stranger from Brazil. He was buying a gift for his wife, who loved postcards. We talked for fifteen minutes or so. He asked me if I was married, and I said no. I never mentioned Michael. Perhaps, it felt too complicated. But would that have been the normal thing to do on the eve of my engagement—to confide in a complete stranger in front of a rack of art deco postcards?

"Sounds nice enough," Michael continued with his petulance, starting to annoy me.

"Excuse me. I need to use the ladies' room," I said, as I was already standing up. I plopped my napkin on the table and darted to the back of the restaurant.

The restrooms were single occupancies, which allowed me to close off the world and the tension at my table. I closed the top lid on the toilet and sat down, staring at the movie posters in Italian on the wall: *Taxi Driver, The Way We Were, Deer Hunter*. I had not seen any of them. Was I a cinematic philistine? What was the last movie I had seen in the theater? I couldn't remember. Was it with Michael? My sister? Why didn't I go by myself anymore? I used to love the art house cinemas in Berkeley.

I wanted to break down, to release my entire life's regrets into the palms of my hands until they were soaked in my failure. A knock at the door and my own rigidity didn't allow for that to happen, at least not in that bathroom with the Italian movie posters.

"That took a while. Everything okay?" Michael asked, his tone shifting from anger to concern.

I returned to the earlier version of myself, before the bathroom and after ruining the surprise. I smiled widely, took a sip of wine, and reached my hand across the table to touch Michael. As we clasped hands, I felt the damage being slowly repaired. It would take more massaging, but, by night's end, we'd have the humming engine of our post-engaged relationship intact.

"I love you, Michael. I'm sorry. You know I just hate surprises."

"To be honest, this stuff kind of stresses me out," Michael laughed, relaxing into himself for the first time that evening.

"So where's the ring? Is it coming in my tiramisu?"

We both laughed, heartily and harmoniously, reminding us of who we were and who we were not. As our dinners were served, we ordered another bottle of wine. The evening took a bright turn, as if it were just another date without any loaded expectations or life-changing aftereffects. I left the girl sitting on the toilet in the bathroom behind, burying her beneath the excitement of a wedding and life as Mrs. Chizeck.

It wasn't until the next afternoon that I put the ring on my finger. I had it in its case on my nightstand, and I kept eyeing it every time I went in and out of our bedroom. Or, maybe it was eyeing me, wanting to attach itself like a small magnet on the refrigerator. Only this was the most significant magnet, not just a reminder of the pizza delivery phone number or the recyclables calendar. This would sparkle and shine, then fade, for the rest of my life.

Michael had gone into the office, as he often did on Saturdays, and I had spent the day busily cleaning, out of distraction more than necessity. I dusted blinds, scrubbed toilets, wiped down tables, and ignored Nancy's phone calls. Despite our engagement evening ending well, I couldn't completely dust off my experience in the bathroom. What if I had stayed and let myself feel whatever was trying to surface? Once I had exhausted all cleaning chores, I took a walk around the block, trying to visualize the life of other couples on our street. How long had they been married? Were they happy? Did the women still care for themselves? When I came to the corner, a couple came out of my blind spot with their golden retriever, causing me to flinch. They were a retired couple; I had seen them walking before, always with the same happy dog. They smiled, initiated pleasantries and apologized if their dog got too close. This time was no exception, as they apologized sincerely for startling me and then told me to "have a wonderful afternoon." They clasped hands as they continued past me, and I could see the tender squeeze of gratitude between them.

I stood there for several minutes, smiling and again drowning doubt. I walked briskly back home, put on my ring, and called Nancy back. She was thrilled, as expected, and that comforted me. She started throwing out all kinds of ideas for the reception and shower and mentioned all the things she did wrong for her wedding. I just let her talk mostly, as I lay back on my bed and stared at the elegant magnet now permanently stuck to me.

The next night, Michael and I had my parents over to make the announcement. Michael had not gone the traditional route of asking my father for my hand, but this seemed the modern equivalent: tell the bride's parents before everyone else. Except the bride's sister, of course. I was making up wedding etiquette in my head.

"Oh, the place always looks so lovely," my mother gushed, as she always did when entering someone's house. She had on a gray pantsuit with red accessories—elegant and tasteful, the standard for Jessica Williams.

"Thanks, Mom. Hi, Dad." I reached over to hug each of them individually. Michael was in the kitchen opening a bottle of wine.

After taking their coats, I led them into the living room. I had placed some mixed nuts with dried fruit on the coffee table, a snack I had enjoyed on a flight with Michael earlier in the year. My father plopped on the larger of the two sofas, confidently, and reached for a healthy handful of the mix.

"Is that pineapple?" he asked with clear distaste.

"Oh, yeah, it's a tropical mix. Sorry, I forgot. It actually isn't my favorite, either," I apologized and immediately thought of something else to replace the mix with as Michael entered with a tray of wineglasses each filled with a chilled Sauvignon Blanc. I could tell by the color; it was one we drank often.

"Hi, Arnie. Hi, Jess," Michael said casually as he set the tray down on the coffee table, next to my ridiculous attempt at creative appetizers. Michael was very comfortable with my parents; in some parallel universe, he probably would have been their perfect son.

My mother sat herself next to my father and tasted the nuts and dried fruit combo.

"Oh, Sarah, that is not bad at all. It's like a little taste of Hawai'i," she giggled.

Michael and I looked at each other for direction, and then he sat down at the other sofa across from my parents, prompting me to do so with his eye contact. He continued to take control of the evening.

"Well, thanks for coming over on such short notice. We're really glad you're here," he talked as he handed out the wine glasses. When the four of us each had our glass, I thought he'd make a toast or something. I thought it might be uncomfortable, superficial. Plus, they were my parents.

"I think what Michael is trying to say," I interrupted, "is that we have something very special to share with you." I, then, extended my hand to reveal my ring. No more words were necessary.

My mother's face lit up. She took a gulp of her wine and then started to tear up. My father just looked relieved. Michael turned to me, surprised but not angry. He, then, raised his glass to have the final word.

"To your daughter and my future wife."

It was nice, simple. We all clinked our glasses together and drank in the moment.

"Here I thought you just wanted to see us," my father joked.

"Oh, honey, don't joke," my mother slightly chided.

I looked across at both of them, seeing their excitement—and relief—about my future. I watched them look at each other, and then drink, and then look at each other again. Did Michael and I do that? I turned to him and squeezed his hand.

"We wanted you to be the first to know," I said, while looking at Michael, releasing my hand from his and then using it to run fingers through his hair.

"I'm so happy. Just so happy." My mother was now in tears as she spoke. My father comforted her by placing his hand on her knee. I looked down at his wedding ring, worn and dull from the many years worn. I stood up, as though I had another announcement. Everyone looked at me.

"I'm just going to check on dinner. Chicken parmesan sound okay?"

"Yum. Sounds delicious. Oh, we are going to have so much to talk about! When are you thinking?" my mother beamed.

"Next September," Michael blurted out, the first I had heard of any dates.

I excused myself to the kitchen, after topping off my wine glass. I opened the oven to check on dinner, heat blasting into my face. I started to sweat. I took another sip of wine, surprised to see my father appear by the refrigerator.

"What's up, Dad? Need something?"

"I just wanted to talk to you in private."

"That sounds grim, Dad." I tried to avoid the awkwardness that was happening.

"Sarah, I know I've been hard on you in the past. I may have hurt your feelings...about your major, your...choices in life."

I could see him searching, digging for the right words. His face twitched, and he seemed to have a slight shake about him.

"Dad, it's okay. I knew you just wanted to look out for me."

"Yes, and I just want to tell you now...in this moment...I've never been more proud of you."

After he said this, he seemed to have conquered his nerves. He had unloaded, seeking some type of redemption, or maybe it was his final approval of my life. Proud...interesting choice of words.

"Proud? I didn't do anything," I said carefully.

"Yes, Sarah...you did. You chose your life."

He leaned toward me, inching closer, and then kissed my forehead. He hadn't shown that kind of affection in years. His eyes were glassy, the closest he'd ever come to emoting. He left me to finish taking care of dinner. I looked down at my left hand, stunned at the idea of making him so proud by simply putting a ring on my finger.

Chapter 5

〜

Less than twenty-four hours after our dinner-turned-sex date, we found ourselves back at Hale Nani for another outdoor dinner together. I had intended to search out other restaurants, but I wanted to avoid the front desk area. Seeing Kalei was dangerous, exciting, unfamiliar. Instead, I spent another day in the hotel room, updating Nancy, checking emails, and reading the *Cosmopolitan* Kalei had picked out for me. I searched for his scent as I flipped through the pages, like a thirteen-year-old girl with a camp crush, and read about losing back fat.

"So, here we are again," Michael said, as he took a sip of his local beer. His face was considerably darker after three days on the golf course. Meanwhile, I had not changed.

"Yes, is this okay? I just thought we had such a nice time last night," I said, trailing off toward the end of my sentence.

"We are here for another ten days, babe. And to be honest, I could eat here every night and be happy."

Michael was relaxed, tan, exuberant. He was everything a honeymooner ought to be—radiant, like everyone told me on my wedding day. I hoped he would soon infect me with this Big Island bug. I wanted to join him, to stop hiding, stop lying.

"Just water?" Michael noted I hadn't ordered a cocktail yet.

"For now, I think."

"Is everything okay?" Michael was starting to notice something.

"Yeah. Why?" I made a point to throw the words away like week-old takeout.

"I don't know. You just seem...off."

"Because I'm not drinking?"

"No, it's just...What did you do today?"

Michael was starting to penetrate, working his way underneath my buzzing skin. My knees started to shake under the table. I thought of how I spent the day, and how I should have spent the day—or, at least, how a honeymooner wife should have spent the day.

"After you left, I relaxed in the room for a bit and then called Nancy." I began the story, hoping to embellish along the way.

"How's she doing? Did you send her pictures?" Michael asked with pride.

"Yes, I sent her some pictures. I, then, checked email, and you know how that goes...a few hours later, I was ready for lunch."

"So, did you ever make it to the pool?"

"For a little bit." I started the embellishment—or outright lying—at that point.

"Good. I want to see the tan lines." He smiled, seeming satisfied with my account of the day.

"You know what? I think I will order a cocktail. I'm going to go up to the bar. Service seems slow tonight." I got up and quickly walked across to the bar, feeling like I had just made it out of a pregnancy scare.

The island bar was situated in the middle of the outdoor seating area, a slightly more elegant version of the classic tiki bar. The thatching on the roof was subtle, and the tiki torches sticking out on the sides were made of bronze. There was one bartender, a woman about my age, scurrying back and forth between customers, who were standing or sitting at the bar. I decided to take a seat while I waited and study the bartender. She looked to be of mixed ethnicity—perhaps Filipino and something else? I admired her agility as she smoothly set down drinks, scooped up credit cards, and ran receipts while shaking more drinks. I wondered how she got the energy. Too many dinner guests in my house overwhelmed me.

The customers ranged from middle-aged couples in Hawaiian shirts to twenty-somethings slamming Jägerbombs and trying to speak

Hawaiian. I was sitting there, somewhere in between capricious youth and the measured pace of middle-aged life. Waiting at the bar, my mind became lost in creating a backstory for the bartender; she finally caught her breath and attended to my side of the bar.

"Aloha. Sorry for the wait. What are we drinking?"

"Hi. No problem. I'm in no hurry."

"Island time, right on. First time to the Big Island?"

I noticed wrinkles around her eyes, incongruous to her youthful demeanor and perky ponytail. I wanted to ask her age.

"Yes, first time. Honeymoon." As soon as I said it, I wished I could hit a recall button.

"Congratulations. We get a lot of you here. You're kind of our bread and butter."

I felt the audible equivalent to an emoticon smiley face at the end of her sentence, and wished I had something to reciprocate the warmth of her presence.

"So, drink?"

"Oh, right. What do you recommend?" I knew I was keeping her from other customers, but I wanted to linger a bit more, drinking in her confidence and ease.

"Do you like fruity drinks?"

"Sure," I said, not thinking about the question.

"Be right back."

I watched her glide to a work station with blenders, ice, and a series of plastic bottles that appeared to contain juice. She effortlessly tossed the ice and unmeasured amounts of juice into the blender before grabbing four different bottles of alcohol. Like some sort of bartender champion, she turned all four bottles upside down at once and let the booze flow into her potion, then instinctively turned all four bottles upright. I had watched bartenders make cocktails before, but never with such flair. I'd heard of places that featured such acts, but Michael and I also dismissed them as "cheesy" or "too corporate." I can't even remember why we formed this judgment, other than an obligation to be in moral parallel to our peers.

In a few seconds, I was handed a hurricane glass full of a mango-colored frozen beverage with a pineapple wedge, cherry, and parasol sticking out.

"Thanks. Wow." I laughed at the ridiculousness of the drink, embarrassed to be seen, almost ashamed.

"Running a tab? Charge to room?"

"Oh, charge to room would be great."

I gave her my room number, and she ran up a receipt for me to sign while I sipped my adult slushy. I suddenly had my first case of brain freeze since high school prom when I had my first daiquiri and lost my virginity. I remembered the brain freeze more vividly than the rest of it.

"Have a great vacation. Aloha." She set down the receipt on a tray with a pen and winked at me, another emoticon.

After adding a 40 percent tip, I signed the receipt and slid it toward the inner edge of the bar. I took a few more sips, enjoying the alone time. Going back to the table with Michael would escalate the embarrassment and shame. He was in a perfect paradise, and I was trapped in a hotel room, shoving desserts down my mouth along with feelings of inconvenient desire. How could I tell him I had achieved the best orgasm of my life that afternoon, and, in the moment of climax, I was picturing not my husband but the young man at the concierge desk? I had tried to keep the pleasure contained, a repeat of my first afternoon delight. But the more intense things got, the more I felt myself visualizing Kalei, on top of me, my hands running down his sweaty back, his tongue all over me.

I had spent the moments after in tears, in mourning for the purity of my romantic thoughts. I then showered, ordered room service, and tried to distract myself with cheesecake and truffles. However, it was too late to turn back on my sensual revolution. The burst of flavor in my mouth just brought me back to Kalei's arms, his body, and the idea of us discovering each other's every last erogenous zone.

"What took you so long? I was getting worried."

I returned to see Michael sipping another beer, his brow furrowed for the first time since we arrived.

"Sorry, the bar was really busy. Had to wait. For my drink, you know."

I sat down, nervously, and took huge sips of what was now becoming the perfect cocktail.

"What are you drinking?" Michael asked, questioning my spontaneity.

"I don't know the name of it. Do you want a sip? It's really tasty."

"Are you sure you're okay, Sarah?"

I felt my palms begin to sweat, the panic in my chest about to spew out of my mouth in word choices I had no control over.

"I think I might be allergic to something," I blurted out.

"What? Here?"

"Yeah. I don't know. I think that's why I didn't do much today. Felt sluggish, but then guilty for not taking advantage of all this...does that make sense?"

"I guess. But what would you be allergic to? That seems kind of random."

Michael relentlessly tried to arrive at the bottom of my erratic behavior. Did he want me to admit to having spent the afternoon fantasizing about another man?

"Let's go back to the room," I said.

"Now? We haven't even ordered."

Michael's concern was moving quickly toward annoyance.

"We can eat in bed later," I whispered, hoping to distract him with some romance. I was in the mood again.

"I'd really like to finish our dinner, Sarah."

"So, you don't want to take me back to bed?"

I had never talked like this before—surprising myself even more than Michael. Michael just looked at me, aghast, his face somewhere between disappointment and disgust.

"I'm sorry. I think this drink is just making me..." I couldn't even finish the sentence. What was I supposed to say? Horny?

Michael picked up a cocktail napkin on the table and wiped his left cheek. There was nothing there. He switched the napkin into his left hand and then crumpled it into a ball.

"It's just...you've been so different about sex on this trip," he said to me while still looking at the napkin.

I had a choice to respond, to reclaim some of the power. I had a voice, a body, sexuality. But I also had a man who loved me, who was genuinely concerned about my ostensible descent to nymphomania.

"Michael, I'm sorry. It's just been the sun and drinks and...you're right. It's probably just like I feel I should be the sexy wife on the honeymoon or something."

Michael smiled, relieved and satisfied with my response. He reached his hand across the table and squeezed mine.

"You don't have to be any different. I married you for the normal version of you, not some sexy magazine model version. I could get that in the gift shop."

We laughed. I had avoided another moment of doubting myself. A warm breeze brushed against my back, a note of acceptance from my surroundings. I would get through this vacation, and everything would be normal again. I looked forward to the fog and gloom of San Francisco, and putting away our wedding gifts.

After picking at a salad and watching Michael inhale a scallop risotto, we returned to our suite. Would we be making love tonight? I decided not to initiate anything, trying to quiet any desire left in me from my afternoon pleasure retreat. It turned out Michael wasn't in the mood anyway. He went to bed with a stack of magazines and his smart phone, a solid signal that he was not feeling amorous. I took my time with my nightly facial ritual—cleaning, moisturizing, staring. As I turned off the bathroom lights, and finally made my way to the bed, I hoped Michael would be asleep. It was time to put an end to the chaos of today and to start the clock over with more control. I hoped for rain, long sleeves...nothing to do but think about going home.

Michael had indeed drifted off. I found him with an *Entrepreneur* magazine opened on his chest and phone by his ear: ambition colliding with peace with privilege in the background. I didn't disturb him, letting the portrait remain next to me as I slid into bed. I turned away from him, staring out at what I could make out as the sea, blackness flowing at a constant pace. I laid there, with no thought or purpose for my gaze, for two hours. Michael remained in peaceful slumber while I remained still in form, but frenzied in spirit. I tried counting, making mental lists, thinking of home. Nothing would bring me under. I relocated to the living room, slouched on the sofa, watching the hotel's resort information channel with no sound. A loop of features with interviews streamed before me, blurring together until, at one point, I recognized a face. It was the bartender from earlier. I walked closer to the television, notching up the volume. She was talking about the signature cocktails and flair bartending. She held the same casual confidence I had experienced with her, her hair in the same simple ponytail and the slight wrinkles when she smiled. Angela was her name. *Angela.*

I turned off the television, returned to the couch, and worked on my backstory for Angela. She had married young, maybe had a few kids somewhere in the Midwest. Maybe Wisconsin. The marriage fell apart, maybe her husband left her for another woman. Angela would love the cliché biography, I thought. How did she end up here? Why bartending? Did she bring her kids? Was she involved with anyone? Did she earn enough to support herself? Did her husband pay any kind of child support or alimony? Did she have friends here? Light poured into the room as I remained on the couch, thinking about Angela and her life. I would wait for Michael to wake before moving, fixating on a woman I hardly knew, fascinated by the possibilities of how she lived her life.

Chapter 6

~

The next day, I started over. There would be no time spent alone in bed, no dessert carts, no touching myself. I started the day by ordering a sensible breakfast for the two of us instead of the ostentatious buffet: toast, coffee, juice, fruit and oatmeal. Michael didn't seem to mind, and we ate it out on the balcony together, a pleasant start to the day and to the rest of my time in paradise.

"I think I'll check out the spa today. And the shops. Maybe go for a walk down by the beach," I announced proudly over my second cup of coffee. I would not go back to bed.

"Glad to hear you're ready to be on vacation." Michael did not seem particularly concerned about me, which surprised and confused me.

"Michael, I'm sorry about last night. I felt so awful about everything, I ended up coming out here and slept on the couch."

Michael had just put a slice of mango in his mouth; the sliminess of it slid down his throat without need for chewing.

"Babe, don't worry about it."

There would be no more discussion about the night before, not today. Before he headed out to the course, I kissed him, tasting the mango and not wanting him to golf. I should have told him that, I thought.

I packed my bag for the pool—magazines, brochures, bottle of water, sunscreen—but I started my itinerary with the walk. There was no particular destination; I merely positioned myself toward what felt like the ocean. Beyond the grounds of the resort, the bright green manicured grass turned to broken lava rock and weeds. The resort was set above the beach, but there were small rocky trails leading down to it. I considered my sandals and the likelihood of something going wrong, but forged ahead. For the first time on this vacation, I felt the ability to breathe real air. The beach was postcard-perfect, white glistening sand stretching for miles against glassy blue water. A group of teenagers had set up camp right at the bottom of the trail, beach towels spread out and radio blasting what I presumed to be local music. I made my way past them, avoiding eye contact, and continued up the shore. There were no surfers out, but a few kids were bodysurfing in the waves. I wondered where their parents were. How could they have the courage to risk the unpredictable water like that?

After what felt like miles—but probably just minutes—I stopped and set my bag down. I took off my sunglasses and stared out, taking it in and hoping for some sprint of creativity as I had seen so often in movies. Maybe I needed a dock for that to happen. I kept staring and took my sandals off, feeling the hot sand against my feet. Just as I was starting to slide my feet around to feel the warmth at every angle, I reminded myself of today's purpose and quickly put my sandals back on. I kept walking.

I walked and walked without an epiphany. Finally, I reached a rocky stretch that my ankles couldn't handle. I turned around and began a deliberate march back to the safe confines of the resort grounds. The teenagers were now frolicking in the water, a boy and girl locking lips and giggling. Their bodies were lean, their skin a color that sun-worshippers in California could never quite emulate. It was an easy glow, comfortable, emanating that island ease. I stopped and took my bottled water out of my bag and watched them play a bit longer. The couple was getting more flirtatious as they must have felt the water was a blanket covering their busy hands. The boy cupped the girl's breasts as she gave an embarrassed sigh, and, by the look on the boy's face, she had reached for more than just a piece of seaweed. I turned around and walked back up the trail, wondering if they had graduated high school and if I could ever handle a daughter being molested in the water by a local boy.

Back at the resort, I diverted from my usual path to explore a new section, away from the concierge desk. I followed the signs to the

Malie section, which I later learned was the Hawaiian word for tranquil. I opted not for the shuttle, instead making the trek myself as the sun intensified. I had emptied my water bottle by the time I arrived at the Malie entrance, a Buddha statue with water streaming over it into a pond of lily pads. The main attraction of this tranquil zone was the hotel's renowned spa, featured on television's *Travel Channel*. I had looked briefly at the menu in our hotel room, but had not decided on a treatment. A massage seemed dangerous, even a wrap or a scrub could lead to too much physical sensation. A pedicure might be benign.

"Aloha." I was greeted at the spa's reception desk as I wandered in, without commitment, by a young Asian woman, not much older than the teens I had just watched getting busy in the waves.

"Aloha," I mumbled back.

"Do you have an appointment?"

"No. I was just walking by and thought I'd check it out."

"Of course. Are you staying at the hotel?" She had sweet eyes—a flower tucked behind her right ear—and wore jade green earrings that caught the light pouring in from the enormous windows.

"Yes, I am. In one of the other zones. I haven't been out here yet. It's very nice," I responded, picking up a menu from the front desk.

"Malie is my favorite part of this whole place. My name is Rita, and I can help you with any of your wellness needs this morning. I think it's still morning."

Rita's speech was rehearsed and genuine at the same time, a girl eager to do well in her job and yet human enough to understand the importance of going off script.

"Thanks, Rita. When would you have an opening for a pedicure? Maybe the 'drenched goddess' one?"

Rita quickly logged into a desktop computer at the front desk and started pecking away, concentrating earnestly on the screen.

"Do you prefer a man or a woman? I have Charles available now, or else Suzanne has an opening tomorrow morning at nine."

I watched Rita's face, bright and ready, as I spotted a pitcher of cucumber water to the right of the reception desk.

"Do you mind if I have a glass of water? I've been walking in the sun, and it's quite hot."

"Of course. Here, let me pour it for you."

Rita came out from the desk and flowed to the side table to pour my glass of serenity. I indulged in my pause moment.

"Thank you." I drank half the glass and then licked my lips.

"Sure." Rita glided back behind the desk and looked back at the computer screen, poised to enter my name next to someone else's.

"I think I'll wait for Suzanne," I said, finally, as I set the empty glass down on the reception desk.

"Perfect." She seemed unfazed by my response and clicked away again at the keyboard before something started printing.

"Can I have your name?"

"You know what? I should check with my husband. We may have breakfast plans."

Rita looked up, again unmoved by my decision. She slid a business card over to me, smiling.

"Just call this number anytime. Whoever is on shift will take care of you. I will be back here tomorrow morning, too, if you just want to stop by again."

I reached down, grabbed the card, and tossed it in my bag. Rita's indifference to my situation was calming; perhaps, I had indeed found the tranquil zone of this monster.

"Oh, I'm Sarah," I said, reaching my hand to hers, feeling her silky palm. Everything smelled like tea and sounded like glass. I wanted to just stay in the lobby all afternoon, drinking cucumber water and constantly changing my mind with Rita's smooth assistance. Instead, I walked back out into the humid uncertainty. Tucked behind the spa was a sundry shop, adjacent to a circular pavilion with a koi pond in the middle. All the benches were empty, a perfect spot for me to hide and stare vacantly into water. I decided snacks were in order, so I wandered over to the store called *He makana nau*, meaning "a gift for you."

The store was much more souvenir-oriented than the utilitarian gift shop near the hotel lobby. There were Christmas ornaments (plenty

of them), Santas on surfboards, shell wreaths, some type of goose featured in various forms, and beautiful blown glass fish in brilliant colors.
I thought of Nancy as she loved Christmas more than anyone I knew. I
should probably consider souvenirs at some point, I thought. I considered buying the standard chocolate-covered macadamia nuts, but that
didn't seem very local. But why did I even care about being "local"?
I needed to get Kalei out of my head. I put the chocolates down and
moved to the magazine wall. There were some bridal magazines I had
not seen. How was this possible? I grabbed both of them, this time not
so much out of instinct, but of hope. Maybe I could go back to before,
spending the day looking at gowns and etiquette guides, stopping every
so often to eat a cookie or sip some tea.

"Aloha. Let me know if I can help you with anything."

I turned around and looked at the cashier desk—another impossibly
beautiful, young island girl. Her black hair was pulled back effortlessly,
beads dangled against the flow of her peasant top.

"Thanks. I was just planning on the magazines. And maybe some
snacks."

"You like sour stuff?" she asked, excitedly.

"Sometimes, I guess." I hadn't seen any Sour Patch Kids and worried this might be a test, like on those food challenge shows where men
eat silk worms and spiders.

"Here, try these. *Li hing mui*. Dried plum, sour. So good."

The beauty pulled out a package from the featured display right
next to the cash register, usually there to entice you into a last-minute
impulse buy or remind you that your breath might be disgusting.

I moved toward the register and studied the package. It looked
harmless, and I liked plums. I fought the urge to celebrate going
local and just stacked my magazines, along with the sour stuff, on the
counter.

"You getting married?" The cashier beamed as she started ringing
me up.

"Actually, I just did. I'm on my honeymoon. I just like the magazines. See if I missed anything."

She smiled, then laughed, perhaps not understanding my odd behavior. Wasn't it normal to spend your honeymoon by yourself looking at pictures of other people's weddings?

"I want to get married," she said, as she pulled out a plastic bag.

"I'm sure you will someday," I assured her, as I pulled out my wallet.

"I want to get married on Kaua'i, so beautiful there," she said wistfully.

"Oh, is that where you're from?"

"Yeah. I miss home."

"I know what you mean."

We remained in silence as she ran my credit card and placed my items in the plastic bag. After I signed the receipt, I looked up at her, really looking into her eyes. Despite her cheery demeanor, I could see there was a sadness deep within.

"*Mahalo*," she said as she handed me the bag.

"Have a nice day. You'll get home soon."

I walked out of the store, thinking about the girl, about her home island, about my favorite taquería. I parked myself on a bench, pulling out the magazines and the plum snack. I could not remember how to pronounce the actual name. I opened up the package and popped one of the hard pieces into my mouth. The sourness was so intense, I almost had to spit it out; my face contorted as the corners of my mouth quivered. And then I bit down, and the taste and texture shifted. That one small piece of plum candy had given way to an entire experience. I reached into the bag for another, continuing to eat the entire bag.

Having drained my water bottle and devoured the candy, I had nothing to occupy my mouth. I just started flipping through the bridal magazine, not finding any interest in the images of perfectly crafted cakes or women in indulgent gowns. I set the magazine down on the bench next to me, crunching the empty package of sour plum snacks. I stared down at the koi pond, thinking back to the fish tank in the airport and how I longed to be with them, to be unafraid of the deep water, living in a different world of bright colors and gentle sounds. The koi were orange and white, larger than any I'd seen before. They glided around the pond, sometimes speeding up, sometimes sticking their mouths up to the surface for food. They were beautiful. I wanted to capture them. I pulled out my phone to take a picture, noticing I had missed two text messages from Nancy.

Are you okay? Haven't heard from you in a while. I guess that's a good thing. LOL.

Hey, how tan are you? Send me pictures. What do you want for your brunch? Love you.

I deleted both messages and opened up my camera application. The intense sun made it challenging to get a good shot, but I finally found an angle that did some justice to the pond's majesty. I viewed it, saved it, unsatisfied. I, then, had an impulse, one I had not had in years—to *draw* the pond. I reached into my bag, digging for a pen that I knew was in there and for a scrap of paper. I had a print-out of our itinerary, so I used the back of that. I sat there, trying to sketch the outline of the entire pond first. The sun started to blaze down on me, as I furrowed my brow in frustration. What was I thinking? I looked down at the pathetic scribble and laughed to myself before tearing it all up and throwing it back in my bag. It was time for a drink.

Pu'uhonua was the name of the lounge in the Malie section, which meant "place of refuge." The name fit perfectly, as I needed to get out of the hot sun and away from thoughts and inspiration. It was a bit of a hike from the pond, just past another pool (for adults only) and across a small bridge over a stream. By the time I reached the bar, I was sweaty and parched. There was only one other person enjoying an afternoon cocktail, a man, probably in his fifties, who occupied one of the outdoor tables. I bellied up to the bar, letting my bag drop to my feet and collapsed my arms in front of me, as though I were a kid about to take a time-out in elementary school.

"Aloha. You okay?" The strong voice startled me. I looked up to see a thick, solid woman, who looked about the same age as the man drinking by himself out in front. She wore a white flower in her hair, but she was not the dainty, ingénue type that worked in the spa or the sundry shop. Her eyes were disarming, having a shrewd power that unsettled me.

"Yes, I'm fine. Just tired. Need a drink."

"What do you like?" she asked, all business.

"Do you have a drink menu?" I asked, feeling like I might be putting her out as customer number two.

Without changing her expression, she reached in front of me and pulled out the menu that had been staring me in the face. Trying to shrug off my idiocy, I smiled sheepishly and started flipping through it. She hovered over me the whole time, wishing I'd make a decision in nanoseconds. I flipped the pages, scanning for something thirst quenching. Just before flipping the page again, I caught the words "li hing mui" and my eyes focused in on what was called a "Li Hing Mui Margarita Deluxe."

"I'll have this," I said as I pointed to the drink, not wanting to mutilate the pronunciation. I was just not confident in my Hawaiian, even *mahalo* felt awkward when I said it.

"On the rocks or blended?" She yanked the menu away from me and set it back in its holder in front of me.

"On the rocks. Thanks."

Again, not changing her expression, she walked directly toward the back of the bar and started pulling bottles down, vigorously muddling limes with something else. In just a few minutes, she presented me with a stunning light purple cocktail in a martini glass with a dark purple rim.

"Thanks," I said, hoping to get a smile from her.

"You want any food?" No smile.

"Um, no. Just this for now. Thanks again."

Still no smile. She disappeared, tending to the man outside, who seemed to order another round for himself. While she was busy making him another drink, I took my first sip, experiencing that same sour pop from earlier in the afternoon but mixed with the smokiness of the tequila and the bite of the lime. I would have no problem drinking several of these. There was a television behind the bar showing surf competitions on another island, apparently Oahu. I enjoyed my cocktail, looking at the waves, coming up with an empty glass in no time.

"Another?" She was back, still not smiling but perhaps the alcohol made her seem a bit warmer.

"Yes, please. Thanks." I smiled bigger now with the alcohol, as she took away my empty glass and got to work on my refill. I felt a wave of confidence come over me, so I went with it.

"Hey, do you know the bartender over at Hale Nani? Angela, I think, is her name." I had to speak loudly over her muddling and the television.

She stopped, looked up at me as if to confirm that I was really talking to her. Once confirmed, she went back to making my drink. There was no response until she set my drink down.

"No, not really. Why do you ask?"

I took a sip for more confidence.

"Just wondering. That's where we've been spending most of our time. I just discovered this part of the resort today."

I wanted to dig deeper, to get any kind of information on her—her age, years of experience in the bartending industry, her marital status. But I let it go. I liked this bar, and this woman made a perfect drink. This could be my place for the rest of the trip. It was, truly, a place of refuge.

I went back to my drink and the surfing, and the bartender went back to tidying up the bar. A few minutes later came the familiar voice from behind: "*Wahine!*"

The bartender looked up, her eyes lighting up, almost a smile. It was him.

"Kalei, you come for trouble?"

"You know it, Pauahi. How's my favorite *wahine* on the island?"

He didn't see me yet. The two were engrossed in each other, like a mother/son dynamic with a slight flirtatious vibe. But not like it sounded.

Then, he sat right down next to me.

"Are you going to give me an aloha, Ms. Sarah?"

I turned to him, seeing his face again ignited the hot switch within me. I tried to be aloof, disaffected.

"Aloha. Are you off work?"

"Yes, just got off. This is where I like to come blow off steam with my girl here. You meet Pauahi?"

I looked at her for approval; maybe now she would open up about Angela or even smile at me.

"Not officially. Sarah Chizeck," I said and reached out my hand. Pauahi approached me, gazing deep into my eyes, and reached out her hand. Her skin was tough from years of washing dishes. Her nails were cut short. I could smell coconut, maybe a lotion that she applied throughout the day.

"Pleasure to meet you, Sarah."

We exchanged a restrained smile, and then she turned around and started pouring a draft beer. Longboard Lager. It was for Kalei.

"She knows how to take care of me. You tried any of the local brews yet?"

"No, but my husband seems to enjoy them."

Kalei took a hefty sip of his beer; his mouth puckered around the edge of the pint glass. He had the island equivalent of a five o'clock shadow—whatever time that would be. He wore his concierge uniform, his tan forearms exposed. Everywhere I looked, I saw virility. His hair seemed a bit shaggier now, as I watched him run his hands through it in between sips of beer.

"She got you hooked up with the li hing mui, huh? That shit can be addicting."

He was more relaxed now, swearing in front of me, a barrier removed now that he wasn't on the clock.

"Delicious, indeed. How do you know Pauahi? Sorry if I just mutilated her name."

Kalei looked over at Pauahi, who was rinsing glasses and stocking tubs with cherries and limes. He took her presence in for a moment, seeming to drift away, thinking of the origins of their relationship.

"Just here. I started coming in about six months ago. We clicked. She's like my island mama, you know? So wise and no bullshit with her. You know what you get with Pauahi. I like that. Mainland folks aren't always like that, you know? At least, not in New York."

"That's where you're from, Manhattan?"

"Most recently. Acting. NYU."

Now it made sense: his charisma, enunciation, ability to exist outside of his mind more than most of us.

"But I quit all that. Came here. Love it. Never going back to that. Too much neurotic energy."

"You don't miss it?"

"No, not really."

He killed his beer and held up his glass for Pauahi to refill it. I ordered another margarita, and we spaced at the surfing for a while. He asked if I'd been in the water yet and if I ever tried surfing. Apparently, he liked to "catch waves" on his days off, but wasn't very experienced yet. As I started to relax and get to know him more, I felt myself genuinely enjoying his company. I still found him attractive, but it wasn't distracting me from conversation.

"So, what have you been up to so far? Get out to Captain Cook? Volcano?"

"We actually haven't left the resort yet. My husband plays golf every day, and I just haven't found the time to take the car out yet," I said, self-consciously, remembering the genuine local flavor remark from when we first met.

"Seriously?" he joked.

"Do you have any recommendations? We have been to Hale Nani," I fired back, feeling myself leaning into him a bit and then catching a glance from Pauahi.

"I tell you what..." He let it hang there for a moment. "Tomorrow, I'll be your tour guide. It's my day off. I'll show you the real Big Island."

I quickly shoved down images of the two of us making out under a waterfall and came down to earth.

"That's very nice of you to offer, but I really can't."

"Because of your husband?"

I didn't respond.

"I'm sorry," he said quickly. "That was not appropriate or cool. I just want you to see the magic of this island. I enjoy sharing it with people.

It's like taking a kid to Disneyland for the first time. You get that magic back yourself even if it's something you've seen a hundred times."

It was a beautiful sentiment, and very tempting. I wanted out of the resort, but knew that spending an entire day with an attractive man on my honeymoon was flat out wrong.

"I appreciate it. Maybe you could send me a list of your favorite places, and I can tell you about the experience when I get back."

I could see his disappointment, as he held up his empty pint glass for another round. He reached into his pocket and pulled out his phone, an older model.

"What's your phone number?"

Without really thinking, I gave him my cell phone number, and, moments later, it was vibrating in my bag. I scooped it out and saw his digits flashing before me. My friendly banter with the concierge had shifted toward something else, something with documentation.

"Now, you have mine. If you change your mind, give me a ring tomorrow after breakfast. Or else call me anyway, and I'll give you some spots to check out."

"Okay" was all I could come up with, as I thought about instantly deleting his number. I threw my phone back in my bag and finished my drink.

I motioned for Pauahi to come over and told her I was ready to close out, indicating I would charge to my room. She gave Kalei a disapproving look, and then looked back at me, concerned. After the transaction was complete, I felt judged and dirty. I needed a shower and a long nap, to be clean and focused. My plans to avoid sensation had failed, from the burst of flavor in the li hing mui to the charged conversation with the handsome boy with the shaggy hair and stubble. I exchanged a friendly handshake with Kalei before leaving the bar. The same middle-aged man was still sitting alone at the table. That's where I should have sat, I thought.

As I made the journey back to the other side of the resort, tipsy and struggling with direction, a striking red bird swooped down in front of me. I knelt down to take a closer look, and the bird did not flinch. I stared into its eyes, and it stared right back at me, attentive. I shifted to a cross-legged position to gain comfort and startled the bird. The red beauty flew away, ascending to the midpoint of a tree and then beyond. My eyes strained until only specks of color could be seen.

Chapter 7

~

I decided against attending the ceremonies for my college graduation, not desirous of having my name called in front of thousands of people who were fake clapping and yawning. Some art history colleagues and I threw a more intimate "graduation" in the art building the night before, which brought the necessary closure to my little world of slides and theories. I had already scored an internship for the next six months at the San Francisco Museum of Modern Art, though the idea of not seeing my people within those walls every day scared me. What would happen to all of us? Wendy was already packed for her Asian tour, starting in two days with Thailand, followed by Vietnam, Cambodia, and Malaysia. She deferred her acceptance to the master's program. I would miss her. Would she call? As the hours passed that evening, we arty folk layered on the saccharine to our sentiments.

"You are the most amazing person ever." "I think you are literally going to be the most important figure in the art world." "No one has every inspired me as much as you." "Everyone in the department looks up to you more than anything."

Sweetly exaggerated, youthfully oblivious, our words served as implants of confidence to propel us forward on our differing paths. A few would go directly to graduate school; some would move back to their hometowns and look for jobs, while others, like me, would go directly to work in the Bay Area. Filling our solo cups with "Picasso Punch," we lounged on the couches in the student lounge one last time.

Wendy came over to me at one point and curled up next to me, leaning her head on my shoulder. I put my arm around her, and we nestled in.

"Are you ready?" she asked, not moving her head, eyes closed.

Only a close friend could ask something so general, yet so specific to the circumstances. That is the economy of true friendship.

"I think so. Moving home will be interesting. Hopefully not for long."

"Shit. I don't think I'll ever go back."

She was right. Wendy was from Sacramento, and she steadily put distance between it and her life until it seemed too far away to have ever influenced her.

"I'm close to work, close to the city. It won't be so bad," I said to Wendy, a bit strained.

"You're a home girl deep down, though," Wendy replied.

I looked into my cup of bottom shelf booze, looking for a future where Wendy was not right. So I wouldn't be backpacking through Europe. My parents lived just outside of the city, and that was where I wanted to work. Could there be something unpredictable out there for me? There had to be, I thought.

"For now, I guess. But, someday, I think I'll do something surprising."

Wendy laughed, and then nestled in closer. We fell asleep on that couch, waking to the sounds of custodians mopping the hallway floors just outside the studio. My mouth was cotton from sleeping with it open. Wendy looked pert and rested as she ran her hands through her hair. We left the mess for later, wanting to get back to our apartment to finish cleaning it out. We had to be out in two days.

After opening the beveled glass doors to let in the glow of the morning, we were serenaded with sounds of giddy students echoing across campus. Herds of my peers in black gowns bounded across the plaza, smiling, drinking from flasks and cheering for their lives. *To the future, to creating our own lives.*

Wendy and I rerouted to avoid the stampede. As we made our way off campus, I felt myself wanting to look back at the celebration.

"Wendy, do you regret not going through ceremonies?"

"Hell, no," she responded.

"Yeah, me neither," I said back to her.

We walked home and diligently put our college years in boxes. It was the last time we were in the apartment together.

The next day, my parents had a graduation barbeque in their yard. It was a small gathering of my sister and her husband, grandparents, and aunts and uncles and cousins I rarely saw. We sat in folding chairs in the backyard, nibbling on flank steak and potato salad and drinking sparkling wine. My mother had encouraged me to invite my friends, but I did not want them to see me in my new/old home for some reason. Despite my excitement over my internship, hints of embarrassment colored my decision making.

Nancy was twenty-seven, married for two years. I noticed she wasn't drinking—not that it would be unusual for her—but I couldn't stop wondering if she had baby number one cooking.

"No wine today, huh?" I asked, casually, as I scooted my folder chair closer to her.

"No, just water. Have a bit of a headache, I think," she responded, a bit off guard.

"You think?" I smiled coyly and took a sip of my victory juice.

"So, how does it feel to be a college graduate?" She quickly changed the subject.

"So far, so good. I know I'll miss Wendy and our apartment and, well, everything about Berkeley. But it's a new chapter, right?"

"Good attitude. I, sometimes, miss it, too."

Nancy had spent two years at the community college a few miles from our house, and then transferred to San Jose State, where she met the love of her life. Her degree, technically, was in International Studies. But, once she met Brian, she instantly became an engineer's wife.

"Yeah? Ever think of going back?"

"Oh, heaven's no!" Nancy laughed at this, incredulously, as if it were the most ridiculous idea on earth.

"Just a thought," I shot back, trying to match her tone.

"Hey, can I get a picture of my two pretty girls?" My dad interrupted us with a big grin and his new favorite camera. We did our best unnatural poses, and he clicked away, capturing another Williams moment.

"Thanks, Dad. I'm sure I look lovely as usual." I raised my glass as I chided him.

"Sarah, do you want to help me cut the cake?" My father clearly had something to say to me in private. I gulped the rest of my wine and followed him into the kitchen.

The cake was simple and elegant, pink roses at each corner and "Happy Graduation" in red with balloons floating above it, all against a white icing.

"So, what's up, Dad?" I didn't want to stall, as that always made conversations more awkward.

"I just wanted to let you know how proud I am of you, getting into a great school, getting good grades, graduating on time. And now you have this internship."

He was searching for something else to say; I could feel it. There was a big *but* about to be dropped.

"Thanks, Dad. I could have never accomplished this without the support of you and Mom. I am so grateful for that, that you put such value in our education. So many parents, too many parents, don't."

"Of course, we wanted you girls to be educated. It opens doors; it gives you a polish."

A polish?

"It's just...the thing is...I look at your sister, and she's already on the verge of starting a family. She and Brian have created this whole life, a house, everything."

There it was; somehow, I had failed.

"You want me to get married? Is that it?"

"No. Well, yes. Not now, of course. I just want you to be aware of the choices you make in life. This internship is exciting, and it could lead to something bigger and then something else and then...before you know it, your whole life is about work."

"I get it, Dad. I won't become so career-obsessed that I scare off men. Is that what you're worried about?"

He seemed stuck, still struggling to scrape from the tip of his tongue his precise point.

"Just know that, in life, there are many different types of success. And your mother and sister should be good role models for that. Should we cut this cake, or what?"

After his sucker punch, the cake no longer looked pretty and delicious. It now reminded me of my mother asking my father's permission to splurge on the fancy bakery. I watched my dad cut in, destroying the smooth icing, dumping uneven pieces onto paper plates. Tomorrow, I would move back here, back home. Tonight, I would buy my own cake and eat it in my empty apartment, one last graduation party.

Chapter 8

~

The motel had an earthy smell to it. There was a fake plant on top of the TV, which was an older box model. The flame retardant comforter had a faded hibiscus print, topped with matching pillow shams. I looked around for one final sign, something to confirm that what I was doing was not unconscionable, but necessary. Before I could summon such communication, Kalei was behind me, grabbing my waist and kissing my ear. His hands moved up toward my breasts, then up to my face. I took two of his fingers into my mouth, tasting dirt and salt. He whipped me around and kissed me so hard I felt dizzy, collapsing back on the bed. He took off his T-shirt, revealing his lean beach body, a small patch of dark hair on his chest. Then, the shorts came off, and he stood over me in a pair of boxer shorts with palm trees on them. I felt my legs start to spread on their own as he yanked off his last bit of clothing.

And then I woke up, stymied by my aggressive inhalation, suffocated by the lurid nightmare. I had woken up Michael next to me. I, suddenly, wanted to make love, to make the desire stop.

"Are you okay?" he said as he rolled onto his side.

"Fine, just a bad dream." I rolled up against him, hand reaching between his legs. I didn't want foreplay.

"Must have been some dream," he laughed, enjoying my handiwork.

Minutes later, he was inside me, and I finally made my mind go blank. I wanted to be dirty, to demand him to rough me up, but knew it would lead to him stopping completely. I needed to have my own climax, so I let my mind go back to the lurid dream—Kalei spreading my legs and touching me with those same fingers I had just sucked. His body was tight, yet flexible, and young enough to go for hours. I gave in, letting him open me up and then push me completely under.

When we finished, Michael rolled off me and let out a sigh of victory. He hadn't had me that worked up since the early days.

"I think someone is in vacation mode," he beamed.

"That was incredible, Michael. You are incredible." I wasn't completely lying.

Michael kissed me on the forehead and fell right back asleep. I tossed and turned, the adulterous wife repenting with insomnia.

The next morning, we rewarded ourselves with a return to the buffet of decadence, heaping our plates full of breakfast meats and pastries. I dived right into a banana-Nutella crepe, landing back in the familiar: cheating with sweets. Michael was grinning, more than usual, his masculinity in full force from our romp. It annoyed me, but then how could he know?

"I guess we worked up quite an appetite." His grin grew even wider. "I'm not gonna be one of those guys that needs a little blue pill, it looks like." He playfully pinched my arm as he announced his status as lover of the year.

I continued eating as he just stared at me, waiting for a response. Michael, of course, I'm still spent. Michael, you are the biggest stud ever. Michael, I want to spend the rest of our honeymoon with you inside me. That sort of thing.

"What's on your agenda today? Besides waiting for me to come back and undress you, that is?" Michael sat back, pleased with himself.

I looked at him, regretting the night before and perhaps more. I cut into a piece of *char siu* pork with my fork, digging for some sort of intention for another day in paradise.

"I got invited on a tour of the island," I finally blurted out.

"Oh, that's great! Is it organized through the hotel?" Michael leaned back, blissfully unaware.

"Actually, it's this concierge. His name is Kalei. He's the one who suggested the restaurant the first night. Anyway, I ran into him again yesterday when I was having drinks over in the tranquil area near the spa." I started to hear myself and slowed down, not wanting to explain everything.

"How nice of him. These island folks are the best, aren't they? So generous, full of aloha," Michael said without a hint of jealousy.

"I don't know. Apparently, it's his day off, and he said to call him, and he'd drive me around and show me the real, local island or whatever. I think I'll just stay here, though."

"I think it sounds fantastic. You haven't been away from here yet."

"Would you want to come with us? It would be nice to explore the island together, do something as newlyweds away from the resort."

I genuinely wanted him to come. Then, he and Kalei could talk, and it all would seem less of a secret, less sleazy.

"I got a big game with some guys I met yesterday, and then they want to drink scotch in some library bar or something. Take a lot of pictures, and tell me all about it?"

I pictured Michael and two other men in plaid, sitting in club chairs, talking about the stock market, sipping single malt from Austrian glasses. They would take turns reacting to their smart phones, firing emails and texts at them. "Not on my vacation," they would joke. "They just keep coming," another would say. Then, they would show each other pictures of their wives, kids, perhaps pets. The bill would come and each man would clamor to pay. Finally, two of the three men would relent with the caveat that there would be one more round on them. They would feel a bit tipsy after the next round, revealing a "hot waitress" or mentioning the scantily clad "island women."

I needed a day off from myself, from this place. It was dangerous, I knew that. Maybe that was what drew me.

"Yeah, you're right. I'll give Kalei a call when we're done. I'll check in throughout the day and let you know when we'll be back."

We? I said it so casually, like Kalei and I were old friends or something.

Michael suggested I call Kalei right there in the restaurant, to make sure he hadn't left without me. I needed to do it in private. Maybe, if

I waited long enough, he would leave, and then I'd go back to my sad routine. Maybe I'd call Nancy, think about going home and opening presents. Writing thank-you cards.

Back in the room by myself, I sat down on the edge of the bed and fiddled with my phone. I brought up Kalei's missed call: ten digits of desire. I glanced outside, noticing the same type of red bird from the day before on our balcony. I watched as it pecked around for food scraps, simple and concentrated. Disappointed by our lack of food waste, it flew away, off to a higher bounty. I returned my gaze to the phone in my right palm and touched the call button with my ring finger.

"So, you in?" Kalei picked up after the second ring.

"How did you know..." I started and then trailed, remembering he had dialed my number. He must have already added me as a contact.

"I called you, remember? I don't get many calls with mainland area codes. We only have the one for all the islands in the state. We're simple like that," he laughed.

"I like simple," I responded without thought. Had I ever voiced this before?

"Well, good. So, you ready or what?"

I looked down at my outfit, an old pair of jeans and a blue tank top. I wondered about the appropriate attire for this adventure.

"How about half an hour?" I asked, casually, as though I were just finishing up a few chores.

"Excellent. I'll meet you out front, by the valet. I'll be in the junky red Jeep, top down. Don't forget your bathing suit."

A convertible. I smiled at this as I said aloha and ended the call.

Exactly thirty minutes later, I received a text from Kalei: *Down in front. Aloha.* I grabbed my beach bag of necessities, checked myself in the mirror one last time for approval, and then made the descent to my non-date. He was just a tour guide who happened to be attractive, I assured myself, as it seemed the older couple in the elevator silently condemned me.

There it was, the Jeep with the fading red paint. One of the tires was missing a hubcap. The top was down, just as he had said, and, in the driver's seat, he sat, wearing a loose T-shirt, board shorts, and flip-flops.

He looked relaxed, a state I always dreamed of but could never find naturally. He smiled and waved. I took my time getting to the car, careful not to get hit by a valet driver.

"Wow, I didn't say I was taking you to a fancy restaurant, did I?" Kalei must have been commenting on my makeup. I had put just a touch of lipstick on. Or maybe it was my earrings, which now did seem ridiculous, considering he wanted to get me in the water. I had attempted to dress "local," with my floral wrap and short sleeve V-neck over the orange bikini I vowed not to reveal. But then, why didn't I just wear my normal underwear? Was I planning on swimming, taking a risk?

"I don't look local enough?" I jabbed back, as I let myself in the passenger seat.

"No, I'm afraid not quite. Local *wahines* don't usually wear earrings in da ocean," he laughed and started the car. I put my bag at my feet, searching for a seat belt.

"Doesn't work. Sorry," Kalei again laughed, apparently not concerned with safety.

"Seriously? Isn't it a law or something?"

"Been meaning to get it fixed. You okay? You can ride in the backseat if you feel more comfortable there."

What the hell?

"This is fine. Where are we going first? And what's that smell?"

"Volcano. The smell, that's *pakalolo*."

"What's that?"

"Marijuana. Weed. Chronic. Pot."

"Yeah, I get it. I went to Berkeley."

"I actually don't smoke too much anymore. My guy moved to Maui."

I was in a dilapidated Jeep without a seat belt, being driven around by a stoner. Nancy would kill me. I wasn't scared of that stuff, though, as my attraction to Kalei eclipsed all other fright.

As we drove out of the resort and onto the highway, I started to cough and noticed a thick layer of fog. Fog?

"Is this fog?" I asked, screaming over the wind and radio. Kalei had put on his favorite radio station.

"No, vog. You haven't heard of it? It's from the volcano, where we're headed. Must be active today."

Vog was a term used to describe the result of the wind blowing the volcanic emissions to the leeward, west side of the island. It gave people headaches, made them nauseous, and ruined crops. When levels were dangerous, some people were advised to only leave the house if necessary, while others had to wear masks. Here, just a few miles away from my slice of paradise, it all seemed so perplexing. It was like some sort of course correction for too much beauty, a layer of cynical gray hovering over us.

A few miles up the road, people had written names and messages in white shells against the black lava rock. "Aloha" and "I love you" stood out starkly, a reminder that people had been on these roads and moved on.

"I'm taking the low road. Hope that's okay," Kalei said, as he hummed along to the radio. Something about fish and *poi*.

"Sure, I trust you," I said, and then I realized I did.

"Well, Sarah, I'm glad of that." He looked over at me and smiled. There was a relaxed energy in the Jeep with the music, lack of traffic, and wind making it impossible to look perfect. Despite the vog and the stench of pot and lack of safety, I was perfectly content. Had I found my imperfect paradise?

Kalei maneuvered his Jeep with confidence and ease—probably speeding—but I chose to ignore the speedometer. Instead, I looked out the side of the Jeep, down the coast where I could just make out the edge of the ocean, and then upwards to the mountains ("*mauka*," as Kalei said). Occasionally, I stole a glance at Kalei, his arms, his legs, his jaw line. I was remarkably *not* turned on, considering the circumstances and my recent fantasy life. I was just enjoying the moment, which, when I thought too much about it, felt incredibly unfamiliar. I wasn't thinking ahead, wondering, waiting, anticipating, or wishing I were alone.

"Do you need to stop for anything in Kona?" Kalei asked, as traffic became suddenly more intense.

I looked below, and, sure enough, there was a coastal hamlet with buildings and sidewalks. I could only make out a few images at our distance, which appeared to be mostly hotels and condominiums.

"Can we just drive through?" I asked, remembering the couple from the car rental place. "Is the Royal Kona close by?"

"Sure, it's right down below Ali`i Drive. Let's take the scenic route."

Kalei veered right and descended toward the coast, through intersections with gas stations and fast food restaurants. We made our way down to the main drag, a slew of art galleries, touristy shops, restaurants, and many signs advertising "adventures." To my right, I could now hear and smell the ocean, waves spraying the side of the Jeep. Hordes of tourists walked about, eating ice cream cones or drinking iced coffee. To my left, I saw even more, sitting at tables outside of a coffee shop blissfully eating cinnamon rolls.

"Wow. Who knew? This is a lively little town!" I announced.

"Yeah, Kona's pretty cool. I actually prefer the Hilo side. That's where we're going. Less tourism, more Hawai`i," he said smoothly.

He suddenly turned right into a parking lot, almost missing the turn to the Royal Kona.

"That's it," he said, as he circled the car around the front entrance.

On a much smaller scale than our resort, it still held something more elegant in its impression. Large portraits of Hawaiian royalty proudly hung on the wall of an outside hallway. The entire lobby was open-air, with a bridge leading over a koi pond. I could see into a bar with the backdrop being the ocean herself. I pictured the young couple sitting at the bar, snuggling and giggling, sharing a mai tai. It appeared there were two other towers of rooms in addition to the main building. A part of me wanted to ask Kalei to park the car, so we could have a drink, hoping to maybe see the young couple again. But how would I explain not being with my husband? We appeared to them old and out of love when we first met; this would only lead them to believe it more deeply.

"Thanks," I said. "Nice place."

"Was there a reason?" Kalei asked.

"Oh, just...some people I know stayed there once."

"Your place is much nicer, trust me," he laughed, and circled back onto the main road. The royal young couple was behind us now.

We continued out of town, Kalei periodically pointing out a coffee farm or important historical landmark. We went through a few more small towns, quaint villages with coffee shops, bakeries, and surf rentals. Kalei turned the music up a few miles outside of the last town, humming along with easy confidence. I continued to stare out, my gaze not particularly fixed, but motionless. I leaned back in my seat, turning my neck so that my right cheek rested against the head rest. I lifted my left hand to the door, holding firmly as the outside invited me in.

The landscape began to change as we climbed in elevation, palm trees turning to shrubs and lava rock. The climate cooled dramatically, though Kalei didn't seem to notice as he continued humming and telling me about how the Big Island had eleven of the world's climate zones. It felt as though we had entered the tundra; I wished I had packed a sweater.

Kalei flashed a twenty to pay for our entrance fee to the park before I could scramble for my wallet. I humbly thanked him, not wanting to fight him on it yet not wanting to reveal any expectation for him to treat me. He glided into a parking spot, turned the car off, and smiled like a kid at an amusement park.

"Here we are," he said. "Volcanoes National Park."

I noticed several small buildings, sort of a community college atop a volcano. I got out of the car carefully, unsure of where the tour would begin. I followed Kalei as he made his way to one of the buildings.

"This is the Kilauea Visitor Center, with information on activities, a gift shop, that kind of thing. Then, we'll walk through the steam vents, around the caldera, and then finish at my favorite place. We'll keep that a surprise," he smirked as he finished his rehearsed tour guide shtick.

Inside the visitor center were throngs of people, mostly Japanese, snapping pictures and obsessing over a video showing a volcanic eruption, bubbling red lava flowing down the mountain into the ocean.

"Will we see that?" I asked, innocently unaware.

"No, it's not that active right now. Even if it were, I don't think it would be safe. They keep people pretty far away. You have to do the helicopter thing to get a really close look. And then you might die."

Kalei laughed as he said the death part, and I wondered if it were some folklore thing about the volcanic gods. Turns out the local helicopter companies were notorious for crashing.

After wandering through various exhibits, I bought a bottle of water from the gift shop and perused the merchandise. I didn't see anything that Michael would enjoy—no such thing as a Kilauea golf ball, I guess. Kalei had stayed back, wanting to ask one of the docents about the predictions for the next big eruption.

We met back up by the entrance and, without words, communicated to each other that we were ready to move on. He led me down a path about a mile or so to the steam vents, which form when ground water seeps down to the hot volcanic rocks and returns to the surface as steam. The ground was so hot that nothing grew but shallow-rooted grasses, leaving it an apocalyptic scene out of some dystopian novel. The desolation was yet another marked contrast to the generic paradise I had come to expect in every corner of the island. I found myself mesmerized by the steam, the quiet, the bright green patches against stark rocks.

"You're not pregnant, are you?" Kalei asked, without any note of context.

"No. Why?" I snapped back.

"Next stop is the sulfur banks, and you're not supposed to go near them if you have asthma or are pregnant."

"Why didn't you ask if I had asthma?" I followed up sharply.

Kalei looked down at the ground, puzzled by himself, and then looked to me with a sheepish grin.

"You got me."

"Neither."

I let him go, wondering to myself why he asked and if he had some fear that I had been a shotgun bride. Maybe that would make sense to people.

We walked down another path, and, when I began to smell rotten eggs, I knew we had arrived. What made the sulfur banks interesting was the discoloration of the lava rock. The gases had broken the lava rock into clay, turning it to reds, browns, and yellows. The smell didn't bother me. I took my time reading the display boards, learning that the area had been recently redesigned to allow for easier access. And I read the sign about staying away if you're pregnant. I smiled to myself, grateful that I was not giving birth any time soon.

Kalei next took me to another building, the Jaggar Museum. We scanned through more exhibits and then walked to a lookout just to the side of the building. That was my first glance at an active volcano, and, in that moment, I supposed it would be my last. There was no fiery lava spitting up, no red hot trails. It was a rather peaceful scene, the constant churn of thick white smoke floating up. If Pele, the fabled Goddess of Kilauea, really did exist, it seemed that today she was in a fairly placid state.

"What do you think? Breathtaking, huh?" Kalei stood close behind me, eager to experience my experience.

"It's not what I expected, I guess. It's nice: alive, yet not overwhelming."

"Beautifully put," Kalei remarked. "You sure you're not an artist?"

It had been years since I'd written a paper or articulated myself in front of others academically or intellectually. I brushed off the compliment, but it made me a little proud.

After getting crowded out by an unloaded tour bus, Kalei led me back to the parking lot, past Volcano House. It was an old hotel, and the rooms had a view of the crater. Kalei told me the food was overpriced and boring, but that the fireplace had been there since the 1800s. He asked if I wanted to go in, but I wanted to stick with our itinerary. I didn't want to miss anything or get off track. Getting off track would be bad.

Kalei drove us a very short distance, but enough so that the landscape drastically changed to a verdant forest. He pulled over to the side of the road, turned down the music, and told me to just close my eyes and listen. I smelled the damp earth and let the symphony of birds greet me. I opened my eyes and saw them flying everywhere. Kalei knew a few of their Hawaiian names.

"This is beautiful," I gushed. "Are we hiking?"

I could see trails and a sign pointing to a lava tube. Kalei looked impishly at the sign, revealing his surprise.

"I'll go first." Kalei encouraged me as we made our way to the opening of the giant lava tube. We didn't have a flashlight, so I pulled out my phone. I watched Kalei's form turn to shadows and eventually disappear. I hesitated, imagining him falling through an undiscovered hole.

"Are you sure this is safe?" I heard my voice echo as I inched a few steps toward the darkness.

"It's fine. People come here every single day!" His voice boomed back.

I could hear Kalei moving deeper into the tube. I tried to catch up, but slipped on something wet, a leaf or a branch. I lost my footing and fell to my knees, scraping them against the rock, a feeling I hadn't experienced since elementary school when I tripped on my own shoelace while running down a gravel slope. It hurt then, just as it did now. I wanted to cry, more out of embarrassment than pain. What was I doing here in the dark with this strange man? I turned around and could no longer make out the entrance; I was trapped in my own pathetic circumstances.

"Sarah? You okay back there?" Kalei screamed, still completely out of sight.

"No, I'm not. I really want to leave," I yelled back, holding back the tears but not the anger.

"Hold up. Let me make my way back." I could hear his feet shuffling, more assuredly than I expected.

He found me still on my knees, gripping my phone in one hand and holding myself up with the other. I wanted to regain my composure, to get up before he saw me in such dismay. Mostly, I wanted out of the dark.

"Take my hand." Kalei reached down to pull me up. There was nothing electric—this was a completely pragmatic transaction.

He led the way back to the mouth of the tube, and, once we were back in the light, I managed to laugh at myself.

"I guess someone is scared of the dark," he joked, and then gave me an apologetic grin.

"This was your big surprise?" I brushed myself off, looking back into the tube with a flash of masochistic desire to go right back in.

"Sorry," he said. "I just think it's unique to here, you know? Not something you'd be doing at home or in a resort."

I smiled my apology, and we walked in silence back to the car. I looked up at the birds and their luxuriant home once more, the light peeking through the canopy of trees.

We sat down in the car, and Kalei let out a hearty laugh. I looked over at him, immediately understanding, letting him infect me. I let go of something, laughing at not just my lava tube panic attack but at the ridiculousness of this entire day. Who in their right mind?

Kalei, finally, broke the laughter. "Hey, you hungry?"

"Sure, sounds good." I looked forward to my first meal outside the hotel.

It was a short drive out of the park to Hilo, which Kalei told me all about on our drive. It was the largest town on the island and the second largest on all the islands next to Honolulu. It had been ravaged by three major tsunamis, and, after the last one, the town rebuilt itself away from the waterfront. Kalei liked that it was reminiscent of "Old Hawai'i" and again used the word "local." Apparently, cruise ships still came in, but tourism here paled in comparison to the sunny side where I was staying. Hilo got more annual rainfall than Seattle, which kept it from becoming a resort epicenter.

As we made the turn into town, we drove past a fish market named Suisan. Kalei mentioned that it was a Hilo icon, and I admired how regal it looked against the bay; the letters on the sign were proudly red. We, then, drove past a myriad of parks, gorgeous green slopes, and bridges that curved over small streams.

"Here we are," Kalei said, as we finally made our way to the edge of downtown. There was a bus shelter to the right, which was adjacent to a parking lot. Kalei turned in, and I looked over at a woman waiting for the bus. She looked to be in her forties, Asian, quite pretty. She held a reusable grocery bag, so I decided she had just come into town for food before taking the bus back to her family somewhere off the grid. She was very slim, so she probably ate mostly fish (maybe from Suisan) and fruit. When Kalei stopped the car, I realized that my glance was actually a stare and turned away.

"I didn't think there would be public transportation here," I remarked.

"No? How do you think people get around that don't drive?" Kalei responded in a challenging tone.

"Where to first?" I changed the subject.

"Let's walk around, see if something jumps out at us for lunch. Reuben's is great if you like Mexican, and Café Pesto is kind of a Hilo institution." He was already getting out of the car.

The sun was burning, and the air was thick, hardly the rainy colony I had just heard about. We crossed the street from the parking lot and walked to the end of the main drag. There were people selling avocados and tropical flowers for obscenely low prices. We walked past the Mexican restaurant Kalei had just mentioned; after reviewing the menu posted on the door, I decided the food sounded too heavy. The sidewalks were fairly narrow, so I had to make room for mothers with strollers or hippie-looking couples walking their dogs. As we made our way down each block, we passed art galleries, souvenir shops, clothing boutiques, open air restaurants, lunch counters, a health food store, an entire museum devoted to tsunamis, a sports bar, and a high end furniture store.

"So what do you think?" Kalei asked, his face eager for my judgment.

"It's...just like any other town, really," I responded, and then realized that wasn't my intent. "What I mean is that Hilo has everything that San Francisco has, just on a smaller scale. It has art, fashion, food, culture. It's nice."

"You don't have to say that. I know San Francisco has a lot more going on. I have to live in Kona for work, but I really do dig this town."

I really did like the place. I imagined that woman from the bus shelter walking up and down the streets, filling her bag with avocados and fresh milk. Maybe she'd stop and treat herself to a new bracelet and have a cup of coffee with a close friend. There was more to the town than I had expected, which clearly was my complete ignorance of the Hawaiian Islands. I came back from my earlier panic; I was glad I agreed to take this tour with Kalei.

"So, what sounds good? There's, also, a bunch of places up the street. There's sushi, Thai, local."

"Local," I said, without hesitation.

"I know just the place. Let's drive, though. It's a bit of a huff, and I don't want to be responsible if you take another spill."

"I'm fine. I would enjoy the walk."

A few blocks later, I was regretting my decision to walk, as we made our way up a side street. Kalei continued to point out fun facts and landmarks about the town. I was so immersed in his passion for this place, I had no clue how many hours had passed since we left the resort. As we veered onto another street, I started to see the dirtier underbelly of Hilo: litter, empty storefronts, suspicious teenagers. I guess it hadn't really struck me that people lived here, just like regular people do. People went to work, loved, and struggled, just like in California, or anywhere.

"How are your feet holding up?" Kalei asked as we stopped for a traffic light.

"Fine," I said back, with a smile. The sun was starting to make me squint, but I didn't want to taint the view I was experiencing.

"Just a few more blocks," Kalei said as the crosswalk light changed. I let him walk ahead of me, stealing just a little peek at his legs. He had an athletic build, the kind that could take in all the calories in the world without consequence.

After another block, Kalei pointed out the restaurant: A big red sign read Café 100. It looked more like a fast-food restaurant, with some picnic tables to one side. I could see a long line of locals ready for their lunch break.

"Burgers?" I asked, as we made our way to the parking lot.

"Not quite. They have everything, but we'll get what they're famous for." Kalei held the door open for me and winked. I looked back at him when I walked through the door and smiled. He was watching me. It was nice.

Kalei wasn't exaggerating when he said they had everything. The menu was overwhelming, ranging from chicken plates to chili to egg salad. There were specials posted everywhere. I could smell fried fish and started to realize that I was ravenous.

"Let me order for us. You can go grab a table. Anything to drink?"

"Oh, how about an iced tea?" I said back, enjoying the mystery and the date-like nature of finding us a table. I decided on a table the furthest away from the cash register. It also had an empty table next to it, so we'd have privacy. There was a newspaper on it, so I kept my hands busy by putting the pages back in order. I finally decided to look at my phone to check the time. It felt like minutes, but I suspected it had been a few hours, at least. I fished my phone out to see I had a text from Nancy: *What's going on? Getting tan? I need pictures!* I threw my phone back in the bag, forgetting to check the time.

It only took a few minutes for Kalei to work his way through the line and procure our meal. He strutted toward me, holding a brown plastic tray with paper cups and plastic containers.

"Making me get my exercise, huh?"

"Well, I just thought it would be quieter," I said.

He plopped the tray down and sat across from me. The little girl inside me wanted to squeal and commemorate our first meal together, but then the married woman silenced her and tasted the iced tea. It was exceptionally sweet.

"So, are you ready for your first *loco moco*?" Kalei grinned, his own little boy coming out.

"Sure. What's in it?" I asked, remembering having seen something about this on the Food Network at some point.

"Steamed rice, hamburger, fried egg, and brown gravy. Café 100 invented it, and it's the best in all of Hawai'i," he said proudly, opening up one of the plastic containers and sliding it over to me.

It looked like a mess of yellow and brown, but I had asked for local, and I was starving. I dug right in, not really tasting anything at first. After about five bites, the flavors started to sink in. On paper, it seemed disgusting. But it all worked. Kalei attacked his, hardly looking up until only a few scrapes of gravy remained in his container.

It felt like the right time to get to know a bit more about him. It couldn't hurt, I thought, and maybe I'd learn things that would make him less attractive to me.

I took a big sip of iced tea, winced again at the sweetness, and then let out my first question. "So, what's your real name?"

"What? Don't I look Hawaiian?" he joked, taking a drink of whatever he ordered for himself. "Scott."

"So, where'd you come up with Kalei?" I asked.

"You really wanna know?" he responded, making me all the more curious.

"Definitely," I said, not intending for it to sound so eager.

"When I first moved here, I was having a hard time. I missed New York, acting, an ex-girlfriend. I used to go to this sports bar in Kona after my shifts at the hotel."

"To pick up chicks," I interrupted, immediately feeling my face blush hot with embarrassment.

"Not really. I would just go and watch surfing, drink beer. One time, they were playing hula. It happened to be this annual big hula festival in Hilo called Merrie Monarch. The whole island goes bananas for it. So there were all these beautiful women draped in fresh flowers, flowing to the music like a single force. It was like they all needed each other, and, by moving together, they were making something bigger than just dance, you know?"

"Sounds nice," I said, still waiting for a punch line.

"It made me realize how different this place is and how I had been trying to live just like I had been in New York. I needed to let go, give up that old life, and start over. So I went to the library and checked out all the books and videos of Hawaiian culture and hula I could find. I didn't want to just be a tourist, a *malihini*. I wanted to be *kama 'aina*."

"So what does it mean?" I asked, disappointed that he had become more attractive and real.

"It means literally 'a wreath of flowers,' but, in spirit, it means 'beloved.' I thought about where I wanted to be, who I wanted to be. I thought about being able to sort of adorn people, you know, like a wreath. So I started over, took a new name that gave me a connection to the land. Sound corny?" he laughed, trying to escape his moment of vulnerability.

"No, I think it's...it's...inspiring." I stumbled on the word, feeling uncomfortably close to him.

We let the moment linger just a bit longer, as we finished our drinks and piled our containers onto the brown plastic tray. The evidence of our first meal was ready to go in the trash. It was time to move on.

"How about seeing a waterfall?" Kalei asked as he stood up with the tray.

Palpable silence followed us on our walk to the car and kept chasing us as we drove a bit out of town to Rainbow Falls. I knew Kalei felt embarrassed, and I felt like an elitist, but not even that so much. It was like I had no connection, no understanding, not to this island or anywhere. I would never talk about San Francisco the way he had just talked about here. Would I ever know that kind of deep honor?

"Here we are," Kalei said without intonation. "Rainbow Falls."

There was a small trail leading to a lookout. There were only a few people hanging out, including a young man of mixed race and dreadlocks. He was playing a flute. As we got closer, the music grew more intense. He was moving his body as though he had no sight, every other sense fully engaged.

"Oh, no, not this guy," Kalei said, clearly having met the young musician before.

"Oh? You know him?" I asked, just wanting us to start talking again.

"He's always around, trying to hawk his homemade flutes. He's a phony," Kalei said with the most anger I'd ever seen in him. The only anger, come to think of it.

"Aloha *kanaka. Pehea oe*?" The young man clearly regained his sight and welcomed us to his private concert.

"Mahalo, but no mahalo." Kalei cut him off immediately.

"Hey, man, that's cool. Who's your friend? From Mainland, yeah?" the musician said, looking at me both flirtatiously and with condescension.

"I'm Sarah." I reached out my hand. "And yes, I'm from California."

His hand was sticky, and he wreaked of marijuana. I looked at Kalei, trying to steal a secret smile to recognize this guy was off-kilter.

"Aloha, Sarah. I'm Geo. Do you like music?" he asked, putting his hands together into prayer position.

Kalei's frustration grew. "Look, we're just here to see the waterfall. We don't need to buy one of your flutes."

"Sarah, is that true? I make these myself, you know? I put my own *mana* into each one, my own island life force that perpetuates the culture." Geo stood up and pointed to a line of wood flutes that were all painted in various designs, ranging from floral schemes to water, to fire. They were pretty, and, had Kalei not been with me, I may have purchased one.

"Thank you, Geo. They are lovely, but I'm just not in the market right now." I gave my polite Mainlander decline.

"Do you want to hold one?" Geo persisted.

Kalei let out a huge sigh, grabbed me by the arm, and led me around Geo. After a few steps, he let go, and we made our way down a trail. The waterfall was spectacular, but I hardly noticed amid the situation on the platform.

"Are you okay?" I asked.

"Yeah, that guy just bugs me. Preys on tourists. Thinks he's part of the island when he just moved here probably a year ago. He's trying to exploit the culture when he doesn't even understand it." Kalei calmed down as he explained his resentment.

I couldn't help but wonder how Geo was different than Kalei in certain respects, though. They both came from the Mainland; probably both changed their names and had embraced the island culture. Perhaps Geo was full of it, but he seemed harmless. I wondered if there was something deeper, but didn't want to risk cracking into something too layered for a light afternoon of friendly sightseeing.

Kalei changed the subject and returned to being a gentleman tour guide, educating me on when the falls were at their peak for the season and when they would almost dry up. He even apologized for his behavior with Geo, and we had a nice moment together, looking up as the rushing water forced its way down, a relentless free fall. It was at its best, I thought.

After sufficiently absorbing the beauty of Rainbow Falls, we slowly ambled our way back to the red Jeep, everything newly aglow in the sun's slow burn. Kalei's brow had some sweat on it, and he was starting to smell more like him. I took a huge whiff and then turned away.

"Two more stops," he said.

"Where to first?" I asked, still looking away from his glistening form.

"The best part of today," he said. I could hear his mischievous grin.

"Wasn't that the lava tube?" I quipped.

"No, you'll like this better."

As we left town, businesses were replaced by trees, houses, and goats. Kalei turned the music back up, and I found my mind wandering to depraved places again. Would I call him Kalei or Scott in bed? Would I start on top since I'm older? I bit my tongue, pulling my thoughts out of the landfill.

"We're about to get to my favorite road. It's like the jungle!" Kalei talked over the music, leaning in to me while keeping his hands on the wheel.

Indeed, soon we were driving under trees on a narrow road that dipped and turned. Ahead, I could just start to make out the ocean blue. If Hilo town had seemed a sharp contrast to the resort on the other side of the island, this seemed like another side of the world. Everywhere I looked, I saw life: from birds to bugs, to bananas and avocados and papayas just growing on the side of the road. And then there was some sort of rat thing that turned out to be a mongoose. Kalei told me that they were introduced to kill the rats, but it turns out that they have different sleeping cycles—a knee-jerk quick fix with no forethought.

I couldn't possibly imagine what the surprise spot could be, unless we were going to some secluded beach. As we turned into a parking lot off a lonesome street, I figured I had been right. The sign read "Ahalanui State Park," and I could see the waves crashing in the distance. There were picnic tables, showers, and a row of Porta Potties. Yes, we had come to a public beach.

Kalei turned the car off and grinned like a satisfied obese man about to belch after a plate of ribs.

"I don't swim." I just said it, without apology.

"Maybe you'll change your mind," Kalei replied, still grinning.

We got out of the car, and I realized I had not been to the bathroom the entire trip, unless I had inadvertently wet myself during the lava tube fiasco. Kalei had to go, too, so we each made our way for our respective business. I was surprised by the cleanliness of the Porta Potty; I tried to think back to the last time I had been in one. Must have been an outdoor concert or a fair or something. I also savored the time alone, away from Kalei and Michael and the hotel. It was quiet and warm. I was enjoying myself. I liked him. I liked this adventure. I think I even liked this place, which was weird. I hadn't had a cocktail to sway my mood.

Bladders relieved, we made our way toward the beach. I made out a lifeguard, but no actual sand. Kalei turned into Mr. Grins.

"It's a hot pond. It's like naturally heated by volcanic rock or something. Like a natural hot tub. And it's not deep. You can stand up the whole way around." Kalei started in as we came to the point of his satisfaction.

I looked out to see people of all ages floating about in this natural wonder, making me think of some mythical healing pool. Kalei took his shirt off as soon as we made our way to the edge, flinging it over a ledge. I looked away, not wanting to be obvious about my curiosity.

"So?" he asked, prompting me to look at his body.

There was a small tuft of hair on his chest, almost identical to the one in my dream. His stomach was firm, with some muscles showing, but not the crazy ripped Hollywood action hero variety. His upper arms were equally firm, but reasonable. He worked out, but it wasn't his life. Still, he would be the envy of many men and the desire of many men and women. I looked down and saw all the happy faces soaking up nature's bath tub. I made my way ahead of Kalei, toward the stairs that descended into the pool. I dipped a foot in, and, sure enough, the water was perfect—warm, calm, gentle. I had to take the plunge. It was basically like a spa day without the scented candles and overpriced products.

"Let's do it!" I squealed a bit, slightly embarrassing myself.

Kalei's grin came back, and he headed right into the water, submerging himself with so much ease that it was as if he had descended from sea mammals. I made my way back to the ledge where Kalei had left his shirt and tentatively undressed to my orange bikini. I felt exposed at first, but then quickly realized no one was looking. I walked steadily down the stairs, enjoying the warmth of the water against my skin. I could see fish swimming underneath me, which was both unnerving and exciting. I looked for Kalei and began to squat lower into the water, until just my head was above surface. I closed my eyes, letting the warmth come over me. I was in the ocean, technically. I was in the water, kind of swimming. Pride came over me, and I smiled. I turned my face toward the sky, feeling a moment of spiritual prowess. Just then, whomever my higher power might be spit on me; a raindrop hit my chin. I opened my eyes and saw the sky had turned a dark gray. I looked around, expecting to see everyone flee to his or her cars. The drops continued like soft pellets, and eventually a full rainstorm pounded down on us.

"Wild, huh?" Kalei said, swimming up behind me.

"Should we go?" I asked, still perplexed that no one else had left the pool amid the monsoon.

"Happens all the time. It's what's so great. It's the perfect place to be in a rainstorm. The water is always warmer than the rain," Kalei laughed, going underwater into some type of frog position.

I started to embrace the imperfection of everything—the makeup running off my face, the inevitable disaster of my hair, the fact that I was swimming with the concierge of my hotel on my honeymoon. I just laughed. I laughed with gusto, my face big and contorted. My whole body shook as I absorbed my awareness of all that was happening. I never wanted to leave that hot pond, and it had nothing to do with my incredibly sexy tour guide.

I used my wrap to dry myself off, though the rain had stopped by the time we made it back to the car. Kalei had his shirt back on, though his torso was still moist.

"One more stop," he said, with what I imagined to be disappointment. I was disappointed.

Not far from the hot pond, we drove into another oceanfront spot called MacKenzie State Park. I was surprised at the un-Hawaiian name, but, apparently, it had been named after a famous Big Island forest ranger back in the thirties. I was amazed by how much information Kalei retained about this place. I couldn't keep the streets in San Francisco straight, much less their historical references.

The park reminded me of home, tall trees providing shade over soft dirt. There were a few picnic tables and a shelter, but no one else was at the park. Kalei led me toward the oceanfront, to massive sea cliffs he referred to as *pali*. The view was haunting and spectacular: huge crashing waves against dangerously jagged rocks. The drop at the cliff was steep, and I had to stop myself from going too far. Terrified, I watched Kalei saunter further toward the ledge.

"Be careful," I shouted over the crashing water.

Kalei turned around, smiled, and came back to me.

"So you're afraid of heights and water?" He reached his hand out and gently rubbed my shoulder.

"I guess the combination is a little too much. This is really pretty, though. Reminds me of home, the trees," I assured him as he let go of my shoulder.

"My pleasure, Sarah." He hadn't said my name like that before. We were no longer a concierge and hotel guest, or even a friendly tour guide and bored newlywed.

"Thank you. I really needed this," I said, reaching out my hand to his shoulder to balance our gestures of affection.

He grabbed my hand and held it to his heart. The emotion on his face was powerful like the pali behind him.

"Are you happy?" he asked, squeezing my hand, still resting it against his heart.

I unclasped my hand and quickly turned away. I took a few steps, looking up at one of the trees to spot a small yellow bird. When it flew away, I turned back to Kalei and responded.

"I don't know. I guess, sometimes, I just feel a little lost," I replied as honestly as I could be with myself, a dangerous cliff to be on.

Kalei took his wallet out from his shorts and dug around, finally fishing out a wadded up piece of paper.

"What's that?" I asked, feeling more naked than I had in my bikini back in the pond.

"It's a Hawaiian proverb. Whenever I'm feeling lost, I dig it up, and it reminds me of my journey. Here."

I took the worn paper from him and unfolded it. It read *Aia no I ka mea e mele ana.*

"What does it mean?" I asked, not even attempting to read it out loud.

"Loosely translated, it means 'Let the singer select the song.' Whoever the singer is for you, whether it's God or the Universe or the Moon...that is who is looking out for you. Like a guide. So if you're feeling lost, you can know there's a plan for you to get back to where you're supposed to be," he said, then let out a nervous sigh.

"That's nice," I said, handing the paper back to him.

"Sometimes, I can get a little woo-woo," he apologized.

"No, it's refreshing. You believe. It's good." I looked into his eyes. We were both naked now.

He leaned in toward me, and I didn't move. I knew what was going to happen next, and I did nothing to stop it. His right hand cupped my face; his fingers trickled down my neck. He looked down at my forehead, his other hand sweeping the hair away from my eyes. And then he leaned in closer, and I leaned into him until our lips were together. I opened my mouth for more, and he took the invitation. What may have been an innocent peck on the lips quickly exploded into passion, hands running down each other's backs, tongues learning to dance together. I had to stop it; I had to pull away. It was wrong. I was wrong. I pushed him away, startling him, and then bolted toward the car.

"Hey, Sarah. Can we talk about this?" Kalei yelled as I sped ahead.

I said nothing until we got to the car.

"It was a mistake. I'm sorry I led you on. I'm married. I'm on my honeymoon. This is insane." I didn't look at him as I gave my speech.

Kalei didn't respond with words, but just sighed and turned the radio up high. I reached into my bag for my phone. I had no missed calls or texts. I brought up the last message from Michael and responded: *I love you.*

Chapter 9

~

The next day, my sixth on the island, I awoke to my first overcast morning. It had almost been a week, and I had yet to show tan lines. We still had another week until we'd be home, away from scented towels and disturbingly crisp linens. Michael was still asleep, so I quietly tiptoed into the living room, closing the door to the bedroom. I looked around, thinking of all the sugar I'd ingested on that couch, how many of my blank stares went just beyond the balcony. It had all been internal before, teenage ennui, a bored housewife concocting her own dilemma to convince herself she was still complicated. At least, that was how I started to see it, how I began to judge myself. The difference between yesterday morning and right now was consequences. I wasn't just bringing toxicity into my thoughts anymore, but now into my actions as well. I took my shiny, beautiful life for a reckless drive. Before I let this other person out, I was just damaging myself. Now, I had the hearts of two men to potentially fling into the deep end.

On the drive back from MacKenzie Park, Kalei and I hadn't spoken a word. He listened to the radio while I played with my phone. Michael eventually texted back: *Love you too. Where are you?* We exchanged notes about our days, making plans for a late dinner in the room. I told Kalei thank you when he dropped me off, and that was it. I wiped my mouth the entire elevator ride up to the room, wanting to scrub away the invisible shame.

"Good morning, beautiful." Michael came out of the room, rubbing the sleep from his eyes and smiling.

"How'd you sleep?" I asked, looking back at the resort's magazine I had been vaguely flipping through for the last forty-five minutes.

"Not too bad. I think that food gave me heartburn, though. Guess I'm getting old," he laughed.

"I don't feel so hot myself," I said, leaving my symptoms as open ended as the account of my sightseeing trip with Kalei I had given Michael over dinner.

Michael stumbled to the couch, grabbed a throw pillow, and hugged it over his bare chest. He leaned over and kissed me on the cheek. I put the magazine down and looked at him, that bitch Honesty hovering over us.

"What are you doing today?" he asked.

It was as though we were living our normal lives but on a tropical island. Instead of work, he had golf and newspapers. Instead of wedding preparations, shopping, and lunch, I had trays of pastries and flirting with adultery.

"I might go back to the spa," I said, without having thought about my plans for the rest of vacation other than avoiding Kalei.

"Turns out I may have to make some work calls, but I hope to get a good game in with some cool guys I met yesterday from New York. They're here on a conference. Can you believe that? Here?" he laughed and threw the pillow aside, exposing his naked torso.

"Let's go have breakfast together," I blurted out, desperate for something normal between us. That ridiculous buffet had become our new normal.

"Sounds great. Our place?" Michael said with a wink.

Our place. I loved it. In just one week, we had established a routine, a history. That was marriage, not explosive kisses on sea cliffs or lurid sexual fantasies.

We shared a nice, normal breakfast together at the same table as the day before when Michael talked me into going on the day trip with Kalei. I ate more sweets than the day before, piling on the French toast and cinnamon rolls. Michael didn't notice as he periodically checked his phone for weather updates.

I did end up going to the spa, but, again, there were no appointments with women readily available. So, now, I found myself back in the tranquil zone, the same koi pond, the same cardinals, the same gift shop with the girl who wanted to get married. And that bar where I first really got to know Kalei and he invited me out. Why was I back here? My intention was to stay away from Kalei, but the part of me that kept making wrong choices had other plans. I turned around and started walking briskly away from the tranquil zone, and back to my room where I would be safe. I'd spend the day texting with Nancy and planning our gift-opening brunch. It would return me to who I was before the wedding. I pulled out my phone and sent a text to Nancy: *Aloha. Can't wait to get home. Starting to think about the brunch. What are your ideas?*

I clutched my phone in my hand, hoping to get a message back instantaneously. I sped up, hurting my feet as I hustled to my own place of refuge. I looked down, hoping to see a message, still powering forward, when I felt the bony edge of a shoulder collide with my forehead. My phone flew out of my hand; I watched it dance across the path in front of me. I was still bent over, recovering, when I heard the familiar voice.

"You okay? You should put that thing away when you're walking. I see kids driving like that, and I just know somebody's gonna die."

I looked up to see Pauahi, the bartender from Pu'uhonua.

"Hi. I'm fine," I said sheepishly as I fished for my phone. My cheek throbbed.

"Aloha," Pauahi responded with no intonation in her voice.

"You're the bartender. We met the other day. You know Kalei," I rambled on, noticing I had two text messages from Michael: *Thinking of you. Love you* and then *Miss you. Going to end early today so we can spend some pool time together.*

Shit.

"Yes, margarita lady." Pauahi stood there like an immovable statue.

"Yes, they were delicious." I tried to recover from my nervousness.

"I'm heading to open up. You want another one?" Pauahi asked in a tone that almost passed as friendly.

"Sure," I responded, immediately regretting it.

"All right. Follow me." Pauahi moved along and I tentatively followed.

Walking behind her, I considered trying to text Michael back but then remembered my hot and painful cheek.

Pauahi let me sit at the bar while she attended to her opening duties, putting cash in the register, cutting up limes, pineapple, and lemons. I wanted to help, but knew she was too proud to share her duties. I held a bar napkin with three ice cubes to my cheek and stared at my phone, expecting to see a message from Nancy.

Instead, another message from Michael flashed at me: *Hey, babe. Everything okay?*

I looked up at Pauahi taking inventory of the alcohol on the shelves in front of me. I wanted to drink it all.

I texted Michael back: *Fine. Just waiting for my spa appointment.*

Another lie, but it bought me some time to figure out how to tell him everything later. He was making a concerted effort to connect to me. But why now? Was he going through the same thing as I was? Was there a hot young golfer he'd been seeing all these days? Did he feel me drifting somewhere else?

"Here you go, Sarah." Pauahi set down a li hing mui margarita, just as beautiful as the ones she made me the other day. I liked hearing my name. I wasn't just "margarita lady" to her.

"Mahalo," I said, reaching for my wallet. That was the first time saying "thank you" in Hawaiian felt natural.

"No worries. First one on me. My shoulder's apology." She winked and returned to her bottles.

The drink was even more delicious than before; perhaps, I just needed it more. I lifted the cold glass to my cheek and smiled. I liked Pauahi and her bar. I put my phone in my bag and finished my drink, feeling all the enthusiasm of planning my gift-opening brunch fade away like the colors of a cheap sweater after its first wash.

I wanted to linger with Pauahi, order more drinks, stare at nothing. However, I felt compelled to return to my room and wait for Michael. I would text him when I returned, telling him to come to the room. I would tell him everything, and we'd work it out. Maybe we'd make love and take a drive up the coast. Or maybe we'd go to a different hotel and start over. Or even a different island.

I thanked Pauahi for the drink again, telling her it was nice to see her. She didn't quite match the sentiment, but her face brightened a little when she said "Aloha." I avoided looking at my phone as I voyaged back to the other side of the resort, eager to plop down in an empty room that I could fill with my muddled thoughts.

I avoided the Concierge desk, skirting around the lobby to discover another bay of elevators. My feet started to blister as I finally made my way down the hall to the door of our room. I reached for my card key, noticing an envelope under the door. I expected it to be some sort of advertisement from the hotel, a free ticket to the lu'au or something. I reached down and picked it up, seeing it only had my first name on it. I let myself into the room, set my bag down on the floor, and ripped it open.

Dear Sarah,

I called in sick today. I do feel sick inside about what happened, but I want to see you. If you can get away, here is my home address: 72-213 Paradise Ln, Kona. Between here and Kona town. Remember there's a bigger plan. Aloha, Kalei

Kalei's place was the basement of a house, converted barely enough to qualify as a studio apartment. His bed was a full-sized mattress on the floor, milk crates on each side serving as nightstands. The make-shift kitchen had a few cupboards, a sliver of counter space, a rusty sink, and a small table holding both a microwave and hot plate. In one corner stood a slender white refrigerator adorned with colorful magnets, coupons, quotes torn from magazines, and business cards of various massage therapists and spiritual advisors. He didn't own a television or computer, but there was a dated stereo system in the corner of his main room/bedroom. When I arrived, he was drinking a local Kona beer from the bottle and listening to a folksinger wail out melancholia. It must have been the same beer Michael enjoyed at Hale Nani.

I declined his offer of a beverage and remained standing. He took a seat at his kitchen table. He looked messy, unclean, near collapse. He wore a tattered T-shirt; the logo was so faded, I couldn't tell if it was a sailboat or a banana. He had the same shorts on from yesterday, no socks, dirt in his toenails.

"So, you came?" he laughed, seeming a bit inebriated. How long had he been drinking?

"So, this is your version of a sick day?" I returned, annoyed at his indolence.

"I do feel sick, Sarah. I'm so glad you're here." He got up as he said this and moved toward me. I backed away, looking out one of his two windows to a neighbor's rotting banyan tree.

"Why did you come then?" He turned around, frustrated, returning to his beer.

"I wanted to tell you in person. You deserve it. This thing that happened, it's not real. It can never lead to anything. I don't even want to know how young you are, but we...we live in different worlds. I'm married, and I have all these stupid Mainland responsibilities, but that's what makes sense for me. I'm sorry..." I trailed off at the end, seeing his eyes begin to water and his whole face drop into his empty beer bottle.

There was a predictable amount of silence as we both digested my words, none of which I had rehearsed. On the drive over, I kept telling myself to turn around, to go back to the hotel, and just write a note back. I hoped I would get lost, but the directions on my phone were so clear. When I pulled up to the house, I let myself get a little excited. Just for a moment. What if it were like that dirty motel room in my dream? I tempted myself by knocking, I knew that.

Kalei went to the refrigerator and pulled out another beer, cracking it open against the edge of his countertop. He went to this stereo and turned the music off, then sat down cross-legged on his bed.

"Well, I guess this is goodbye," I said it with no intention of leaving. I just wanted a reaction, something more than the defeated little boy in front of me on a bed with no one else around.

"You're a beautiful woman, Sarah. You have so much potential, and I think you know that about yourself."

He said it with a matter-of-fact casualness, bereft of emotion or motive.

I looked at the door, then out the window again, and then up at the ceiling. It was one of those popcorn ceilings from the seventies, and it was peeling off in one of the corners. There were water stains above the bed and a smashed mosquito above the sink. I kept circling the apartment, trying to fix my gaze on the most disgusting elements I could find. It smelled a bit like dirty dishes. I walked over to the sink and confirmed the smell, a piece of moldy cheese stuck to an orange plate and an entire carton of milk just thrown in the sink—deferred cleanliness.

"You don't like cleaning, do you?" I asked, pointing to the sink.

"Not always," he said, without any further comment.

I set my bag down on the table, relaxing my grip for the first time since entering Kalei's apartment. I opened the refrigerator and pulled out a bottle of beer, the same kind he was drinking.

"First drawer next to the sink, there's a bottle opener," Kalei told me.

I cracked open the beer and took a healthy swig. I sat down at the table, noticing grime on the hot plate and grease on the door of the microwave. I took another sip.

"I thought you were leaving," Kalei said, still from the bed.

"Potential?" I asked, taking a third big sip.

"Is that surprising?" Kalei asked, setting down his beer on the floor next to his bed.

"What do you mean? Potential for what?" I asked, killing the rest of the ice cold beer.

"I don't know, I guess…I see you doing stuff. You know, like when I thought you might be an artist or something. It just seems like there's more there or something."

Kalei relaxed back onto his bed, resting his head on a pillow. I stood up, made my way for the door and locked it.

When I finally said the words "I have to go," it was already over. I was looking at him, his face so close to mine, the worn jersey sheets barely covering me. His face was still warm, emanating an intoxicating heat. There was sweat on his lips and chest. One spot after another on him drew evidence of his undeniably fine performance. It was more than the dingy motel fantasy. I wished I could solely exist in the physical for a bit longer, finding the bounty of pleasure points that had eluded me my entire life.

"Don't go yet," he said, trying to seduce me into round two.

"I have to. I need to get back. And I need to stop seeing you."

I returned to the person I kept telling myself to be as I got out of bed with a sheet wrapped around me—a television cliché.

"Keep telling yourself that, Sarah. Keep telling yourself." Kalei rolled over in defeat.

I quickly dressed and grabbed my bag from the table. I realized I was calm, calmer than I had been on the drive over or after the kiss. My head was racing, but I didn't feel like the neurotic tornado of infamy I had predicted if I were to ever go through with it. Still, I knew it was wrong, and even the best sex could not compete with my marriage. I would figure this out, calibrate my actions into an explanation and move on. I just had to separate body from mind, easy enough.

Just as I was ready to give my unruffled departure speech, Kalei got out of bed and walked, naked, to his stereo. I looked up at the decrepit ceiling to turn myself off, but I had been on my back staring at it when he made me happen. Nothing related to him could ever turn me off again. I simply turned around and walked to the door, unlocked it, opened it up, and walked back into my life.

Chapter 10

~

M y mother and Nancy had wanted to throw me three different bridal showers: one for couples, one for close girlfriends, and one for close relatives. I had already nixed the idea of a bachelorette party as the image of me sliding dollar bills down the glistening abs of a fake cop seemed embarrassing for a thirty-something bride. I blamed Michael for not wanting a couples event, and then later announced my wish to combine the two remaining showers, so I could focus more on the wedding itself. After a tense family dinner followed by four days of the silent treatment, Nancy finally gave in and agreed to throw me one very special shower to include girlfriends and female relatives.

It was an afternoon shower, beginning at two o'clock with white wine and bite-sized sandwiches. Nancy exceeded herself with the decorations, which were painstakingly detailed and feminine. Lace dripped from every surface, bowls of pastel mints nestled up against cut-out cookies in the shapes of wedding dresses, topped white icing and edible silver beads. The mantel that usually displayed pictures of Nancy's children and their recent soccer trophies had been cleared and replaced with a photo documentary of my life. To the left was a grainy photograph of my mother holding me as an infant, and to the far right was a picture of Michael and me taken shortly after our engagement. Everything in between seemed like a blur that we no longer talked about.

My mother's two sisters arrived right on time, followed closely by Michael's mother and grandmother. There were cousins, a few high school friends, friends of Nancy's. None of my college friends could make it, and I hadn't invited anyone from my previous jobs. I figured I'd see them at the wedding.

"Isn't this so wonderful?" my mother asked, leaning in as I poured my second glass of wine.

"Yes. Nancy is amazing at this stuff. I really don't know how she does it." I glanced over at another highly decorated table, a display of beautifully wrapped gifts for me to open. It was more than any birthday or Christmas. And it was all just beginning. Some had already given engagement gifts and then there would be the wedding gifts. I knew most of them would come from our registry, which made sense but also seemed a bit indulgent. I guess I just wasn't used to all this attention, all this praise. The wedding would be over in three weeks, and then I could return to my humble self, I thought. I'd write thank-you cards in my pajamas. I'd use my new appliances in the quiet of our home. I'd sleep nicely on our new high thread-count sheets.

"My ears are burning." Nancy appeared, radiant with a displaced effusiveness.

"Thank you," I said softly, holding my hand to my heart as a display of conviction. And I did mean it. I truly loved Nancy.

"Is someone ready to open her gifts or what?" Nancy screeched a bit, like she used to when she talked to her best friend Marilyn in high school. Marilyn moved to Portland and is now living with a woman who everyone but Nancy has discerned to be her girlfriend. They are no longer close, which I know makes Nancy sad sometimes. Nancy is apolitical and averse to conflict, in many ways like our mother. She is just a more caffeinated, involved version.

I watched as the most eager guests made their way toward the two facing couches in the family room. Others followed and sat on the floor while some stood and some used the extra folding chairs Nancy had dragged in from the garage. For a moment, I struggled with my itching desire to trade places with one of my guests, to just sit silently and watch.

I was directed to the special club chair that had been moved from Nancy's formal living room into the family room for the occasion. It was dark leather with squared edges and plenty of scratches. It was not a piece of furniture that even belonged in a formal living room, but it made sense in Nancy's world. Her priorities had shifted over the years. She stopped buying new clothes, barely wore makeup or perfume. Today, she was wearing a new dress, though. She looked pretty in a light shade of violet; her lips were a frosty pink that made me think of the frosting on cherry chip cupcakes. She would bring me my gifts from the gift table one by one, starting with a silver box from my aunt Linda. Linda was my mother's older sister who lived in San Jose with her husband, a retired dentist. She was always bright and cheerful, smiling about something, or nothing. We rarely got past "How are you?" until she broke out into a heaving grin.

I opened the card first, which had a long poem about love on the cover. I pretended to read it, thoughtfully, and then opened a simple handwritten message: "Best wishes to our dear niece." I smiled at Aunt Linda, and she nodded to acknowledge my gratitude. Next, I tore off the silver gift wrap to reveal four place settings of the everyday dishes I had picked out. We actually already owned four, but this would allow us to grow to larger informal dinner parties if the occasion arose. I acted surprised and thanked Aunt Linda for her good taste and generosity. Again, she nodded back at me, and the procession continued. I would open a plush bathrobe, an immersion blender, a negligée, more dishes, champagne flutes, bath towels, scented candles, a candelabra, and throw pillows. I replayed the same gestures with each one, though I was only genuinely surprised by the negligée. It was from Stephanie, the wife of one of Michael's friends. We weren't terribly close, but had come to bond over the years during our double dates. It had been the only off-registry gift, which I think had me more disarmed than its risqué nature. Was it allowable to go off script like that?

Stephanie took a bold risk with her gift. But to no surprise, Nancy won the thoughtful and creative competition. Instead of just picking something off my list—the list I specifically created for my future life—she had to go rogue and put together my very own "wedding day kit." Inside a handcrafted tote with my name stitched in, I found tissues, baby wipes, safety pins, bottled water, and a small mirror. Each item had a gift tag attached that explained its usefulness, straight from a "seasoned bride."

"There are two more, the wrapped ones." Nancy pointed out, as I appeared to be finished admiring each item for its rich wisdom.

I pulled out the two gifts, one a small box and the other a medium rectangle. I opened the small one first, looking at Nancy for a clue. I could tell this was momentous for her, the face full of anticipation, hope, and a raw joy I always wondered about.

"Your something borrowed," she burst out, as I delicately palmed the necklace that she had worn to her own wedding.

"Wow! It's in perfect condition!" I said, holding it up for everyone to see.

My mother and Nancy were both tearing up, and I wanted to join in what they were feeling. I felt vulnerable, my whole being on display for others to scrutinize, closely determining each reaction. The second gift was a silver picture frame with separate photos of my father and Michael placed side by side. There was an engraving that read "the man giving you away and the man receiving you."

My mother's idea of going off-registry was not as sentimental, but equally generous. Inside a card specifically cherishing the mother-daughter bond was a check for five hundred dollars. I can't say I was surprised at that, but, again, I felt obligated to strain bewilderment to showcase my blessed awareness.

I knew there would be a game coming after gifts as I begrudgingly told Nancy it was okay as long as it didn't involve too much participation on my part. It turns out it required none. Nancy passed out pieces of paper and pens to all the guests, instructing them to write down as many things about me as they knew or remembered once I left the room. The winner would be the person who observed me the most, and would walk home with a spa certificate.

I was relieved to have some time alone. I poured myself a glass of wine and headed upstairs. I wandered into Nancy's bedroom, for no particular reason. It was a decent-sized room, with two closets and a full master bathroom. The tidily made sleigh bed looked inviting; I wasn't sleepy, not even tired. It was more like a slow drain of energy, like the reverse of an IV drip. I sat on Nancy's side, setting my glass of wine down on her nightstand. On it were her reading glasses, a book she was reading on life balance, and as many family photos as she could cram onto the remaining surface. There was her wedding photo, baby photos of all the boys, and shots of recent vacations to San Diego and Arizona. That same raw joy oozed out of each photograph, mustering up the same questions I refused to ask myself.

"We're ready for you."

My mother's voice called out from just outside of the bedroom. She caught me staring at the photos; I had lost myself in them for several minutes.

"Okay," I said, looking up at her.

"You okay?" she asked, coming toward the bed.

"I was just admiring these photos, Nancy's family. They seem very happy," I returned, trying to be steady.

"They sure are. Look at them," she said, sitting down next to me.

"Do you think I'll be that happy?" I asked her.

"Oh, please. You're already there." She grazed my knee and laughed.

"Three more weeks" was all I could come up with in reply. I downed the rest of my wine and stood up, ready for the final segment of the day that was all about me. My mother followed, holding my arm as we walked out of the room and away from Nancy's cozy collection of familial bliss.

By the time I was driving home, I had forgotten who had won the game, who knew me the best. The back seat was filled with gifts and leftover cookies. I reached back to grab one, then two, then three. I admired their perfect texture, their impeccable decoration, and pondered how they might taste in a different shape.

Chapter 11

~

When I returned to the resort from Kalei's apartment, I found a scraggly cat hanging out in the parking lot. It was pacing around in circles, crying out for someone to understand. I knelt down to pet it, and it hissed at me, quickly pushing me away. I stood up and tried to calm it with my voice.

"It's okay," I said to the pathetic little thing. "Are you hungry?"

I wanted to get it some food and water, but I only had so much time to clean off my afternoon whoredom before Michael got back to the room. I reached down again, this time just putting out my hand for the cat to sniff. It came right to me, rubbing its head up against my hand. I wanted to stuff it in my bag and bring it back to the room, nurse it back to health, and take it home to San Francisco. We never had pets growing up. When I stopped working, people suggested I get a little dog to keep me company during the day. It seemed like such a blatant attack on my independence at the time, but standing there over that starving cat in the sunny glow brought deeper insecurities to light.

Nauseous with guilt, I walked away from the cat, covering my ears as it cried out to me. I hurried through the lobby, annoyed at the surge of guests checking in. I got back to the room, out of breath, the taste of bile erupting in my mouth. I couldn't get the image of the cat to go away until I focused on Kalei's body. But then the hissing cat returned alongside Kalei's naked torso: two images competing to tear at my psyche. I took a bottle of seltzer water from the minibar, hoping to calm my stomach. I knew a shower was necessary, but a part of me felt I deserved to wear the stench of my own choices. I started to see myself in that luxurious shower, just standing there with the hot water pouring over me, sobbing dramatically until I had to crouch down into the tub. It disgusted me, and soon a cool breeze of disdain began to envelop the entire room—the stupid balcony, the hideous couch, those starchy sheets. I couldn't stay there another day.

Intent on cleansing without histrionics, I undressed in front of the bathroom mirror. I grabbed one of the freshly folded washcloths on the counter and threw it in the sink. I turned on the hot and cold water, reaching for that tepid point where it feels like nothing. I turned off the water, squeezed some soap onto the cloth, and rang it out with hatred. I started with my throat, rubbing gently before switching to my right arm. With my left arm, my scrubbing became more aggressive, until it was painful. I returned to a steady pace, deliberately attacking the filth on my skin. I, then, turned my attention to my insides, which were laden with Kalei. I made sure it was not pleasurable, assiduously scraping every piece of him out of me as though my cloth were a dull-edged knife.

I stared at my naked body in the mirror, feeling clean and dirty, hungry and full. I pulled my hair back into a ponytail, reminding me of my college days. Those women with super short hair always made me jealous; I often longed to have the angular features to allow for such simplicity. Instead, I maintained my mop of brown security, with the subtle highlights furiously applied on a regular schedule by an over-priced man I'd call fabulous for no apparent reason. I didn't bother with makeup or jewelry. I played with my wedding ring for a few minutes, realizing I hadn't taken it off when I was with Kalei. I walked over to the dresser outside of the bathroom, opening drawers without any purpose. I stared back at my ring for a moment, thinking of what to wear to dinner with Michael. I noticed as I bent over to open a bottom drawer that I was sore, a stretch and strain I would associate with athleticism. I drew out fresh underwear and a bra I hadn't worn on the trip yet, and quickly put them on. Bored of summer dresses, I decided on a pair of jeans and a sweat jacket I had packed in case I had felt the urge to exercise. It was one of my favorites: soft, gray, and fitted enough to hug up against my hips rather than slop all over me like an old duvet.

I couldn't stand another minute in that room, my contempt alive in every surface. I texted Michael to meet me at Hale Nani—at least, it was away from the room—for a late lunch. It was odd that we would be spending time together in the earlier hours; the later afternoon always had me anxious in anticipation of what we'd talk about in the evening. I reached into the snack drawer for something, swinging back to hunger from full. I pawed my way around a handful of gourmet chocolates and truffles, fine sea salt caramels, and landed on a plain old Snickers. It was a familiar taste, one I used to know from my early days of trying sports: middle school volleyball, summer soccer camp, a very brief tennis membership. I endured the practice, the pain, the boredom, for the reward at the end. Sometimes, it would be something as basic as sliced oranges, but more often than not we were treated to junk food. My favorites were the chocolate bars. Those first few bites made the exhaustion, the awkwardness, the feeling of failure, all slip away.

As I walked through the resort eating my pedestrian candy bar, I felt alive with defiance. I had no makeup on, no "resort wear" on my body, and, earlier in the afternoon, I'd had my way with a younger man. Again, I caught myself feeling impossibly at ease. I tried letting the thoughts slip away, wishing I had another candy bar to assist me. I grasped the wrapper in my fist. My right hand was smeared with chocolate by the time I made it to the restaurant. I knew it would be some time before Michael would meet me, so I headed into the bar and bellied myself up for a drink to wash down the sugar. Opening my palm, I let the dirty wrapper drop to the bar counter and watched it uncoil into what one might call a flower. Wiping off my hands with one of the cocktail napkins stacked neatly to the side of me, I heard a familiar voice. It was Angela, the bartender from the television. She was laughing, talking to another bartender, and not wearing her uniform. She had on a pair of dark jeans—almost black—and an apron top with a floral design. I tried not to stare or eavesdrop. She was there to pick up a check, it seemed.

I wondered where she was going. Did she have a date? Did she have a babysitter?

Before I could scrutinize Angela's situation in more detail, I was approached by the bartender on duty. He was a young guy, younger than Kalei even, a boy with rosy cheeks and bright blue doll eyes. I tried looking behind him, to get a glimpse of Angela. She was kind of stunning, right there in the light of the late afternoon.

"What are we drinking?" the doll bartender half screamed at me, forcing my attention to him.

"Oh, just a club soda for now," I replied, wistful for that spiked smoothie Angela had made for me earlier in the week.

I hadn't given much thought to ordering a soft drink; the words just came out of me, perhaps some effort on my subconscious to deepen the cleanse I'd started with my sponge bath.

"There you are. Anything to eat? Menu?" The boy set down my club soda, a furious fizz with large chunks of lime swirling in it.

"No, thanks," I replied calmly, seeing Angela wave goodbye to her coworkers and then disappear.

The soda, in its banal nature, was soothing. I sipped it slowly, missing the view of Angela and trying to avoid eye contact with anyone else. I needed to leave this ridiculous place, with its themes and specials and ugly fountains. I disengaged from my surroundings with my phone, checking email and weather back in San Francisco. I had a missed call from Nancy, probably about the brunch I had faked interest in. I went back to my call history and contemplated deleting Kalei's number. I texted Nancy that I'd call her in the morning. I ordered another club soda, and waited.

Michael met me in the bar, and we decided to just dine there as well. He ordered another one of his beloved local beers, and I kept with club soda. Not having an umbrella in my drink made me a buzzkill, but my "when in paradise" attitude had lost all its luster. I let Michael order for us, a series of small plates for us to share. I picked at some tuna, nibbled on yam fries, and occupied my hands with edamame.

It was mostly small talk at first. Michael talked about his golf game, the weather, phone service. He didn't seem put off by my appearance, not even mentioning it. In fact, he told me I looked very relaxed and kissed my cheek when he first sat down. I wondered if he missed the taste of makeup, or if he could even tell. After about halfway through his second beer, Michael became more chatty. He scarfed down the rest of the appetizers, commenting on how fresh everything tasted. It was after he wiped his mouth with a red folded napkin that he made his announcement.

"So, I'm going to take the rest of the trip to just be a husband. No more golf. Just you and me exploring this island." He reached over to touch my shoulder, in his mind an utter validation.

"But it's what you love." I squeezed his hand, drawing it down to my knee.

"I love you more. I know this hasn't been the ideal vacation for you and I want to make up for it. You shouldn't have to go sightseeing with strangers," he joked, casually, as if I had been going on bus tours with senior citizens.

"Actually, I have something to tell you as well." I straightened in my bar stool, squeezing his hand harder.

"Everything okay?" he asked, his face suddenly painted with concern.

"It's fine. I just, I really want to go home. You still have another week off from work, so we could spend it together at home, not even tell anyone we're coming back early. I love you and all this, but it's just... not me." I fumbled toward the end, my voice cracking before Michael pulled his hand away.

"No way! Are you kidding me? Do you know how much this is costing me?" he responded, the various colors of concern melting to an incredulous red.

"I know. I'm sorry!" I leaned in toward him, not wanting to draw attention to us, the lone, unhappy couple.

Michael drank the rest of his beer in silence, before ordering a final round and requesting the check. I stared at him, hoping to elicit a friendly response—one that ended in "Let's go home." It was the only way for us, I thought. My body was different. Things tasted differently, felt differently. I needed to go back to a routine, to making lists and appointments. Whatever was waking up had to be put to sleep, and distance seemed the only method.

Finally, after taking the last sips of his beer and signing the bill, Michael spoke to me. "I'd actually like to stay longer. I was thinking about it. I love it here. I could easily telecommute. What if we bought a condo or a vacation home?"

I did not respond as Michael got up, signaling me to follow him back to the room. What if I told him the truth? Would he seem so in control then?

Silence followed us back to our room, which had become a closet full of shadows in the pre-dinner hour. Guests were just waking from their afternoon naps, beginning to stir together dinner plans with the sun-kissed excitement dripping from their sleepy eyes. I walked out to the balcony, creating a boundary as I leaned over the edge and looked anywhere but back inside. Michael didn't follow me; I could hear him rustling newspapers and kicking off shoes. I only knew how to be quiet, to be wrong, to wrap myself in an invisible shawl of guilt.

I could hear the shower, and, for a moment, I considered walking out. I would take the car and drive into town, walk up and down the streets filled with shops and eateries, with no direction. Maybe I'd just keep driving around the island until the hours turned to days, until it was time to board our plane back home. But I stayed in that room, waiting for my husband. Thinking back to what made Michael happy, I studied the room service menu and scanned the scotch list. I found one he loved and ordered a bottle. The shower stopped as I ran through the list of in-room movies, searching for his favorite genre: the blow up film. Or, to be fair, it was his favorite genre that I never watched with him. I found a few he hadn't seen yet (because of me) and selected them to view. Michael glided out of the room, relaxed and shiny, wearing a crisp white robe. It was the best he had looked to me the entire trip—tactile, accessible, an easy sex appeal that I didn't always notice. But my attraction was academic, cerebral. It lacked the throb that slowly scattered my thoughts— the throb that deliberately plucked my feathers and then set them adrift in a confusing wind.

The doorbell rang. I flinched, startling Michael, and then fled to the door. I signed for the scotch, then wheeled it in on its cart. Michael came out of the bedroom, seeking out his surprise.

"What's this?" he asked, a smirk on his face as he recognized the label and its worth.

"I just wanted to surprise you. I know it's your favorite." I talked sheepishly, not framing it as a blatant apology.

"Thank you," he smiled widely.

I continued wheeling the cart into the bedroom, which Michael discerned as an invitation more intimate than movie watching. He poured himself some of the fine scotch, savoring and swirling. After finally swallowing, he set the glass down on the cart and leaned in for an emphatic kiss. I guided him toward a firm hug, keeping him close.

"There's another surprise," I winked, walking toward the television in the bedroom.

Michael watched me carefully as I fumbled with the remote to get back to the movies I had just selected. When I finally won my battle with nerves and technology, he let out a familiar laugh.

"We're watching blow up movies?" he asked in happy disbelief.

"Yes, I hope you like your surprises," I said, suddenly meek.

"I love you." He spoke honestly, coming toward me again but this time for comfort instead of passion.

We curled up in bed and started the first movie, holding hands at first until it became too awkward. I had a sip of Michael's scotch, but I wanted to make sure he drank most of it. He had a ball, getting drunk and reveling in the mastery of the car chase. He passed out before the second movie ended, flat on his back with one hand clutched to a full glass of scotch. I pried it away, turned off the movie, and tucked him in. I felt relieved in the stillness, in making it through another day on the island, another night at the hotel. I wondered if I would ever really be with Michael again. If not, how could I make it be normal? I went back to the balcony and shut the sliding glass door, sealing myself off from the room and all its intention.

Much later, I slipped quietly back inside, a burglar among my own possessions. I sat on the couch, not taking any risks in awakening Michael. I'd be gone by the time he woke up, his pounding head distracting him from my whereabouts. I thought of what might be open in the middle of the night. Carefully, I moved my shoes next to the front door and tucked essentials into my bag. The clock on my phone said nine-thirty, but it felt like the middle of the night. I didn't go back to the room to look at Michael; I slid out into the night: face unpainted, spirit unhinged. The moonlight gently guided me to the rental car, where I found small pieces of dried cat food. Someone had fed the stray.

I called out to it.

"Kitty, here, kitty."

I kept my voice low.

Searches in nearby shrubs were fruitless. Disappointed by the lack of apparition, I resolved to get in the car and drive somewhere. Anywhere. In the dark, the island was a disorienting darkness with an echo of unfamiliar sounds. Using every headlight I could find, I made my way out of the resort to the main road. I could go left or right, the latter the path I already knew.

Thirty minutes later, I found myself seated at a bar, the black ocean just beyond the glowing liquor bottles. A woman came up to the bartender asking if he had any Jägermeister yet. He responded that they were still out of stock, but he could offer something similar. The woman and her friend cackled together and declined his offer. They were dressed up, appearing to grasp for a different time in their lives. They kissed the bartender goodbye, clearly on familiar terms with the guy.

"Sorry about that," he said to me, setting down a coaster next to my phone.

"Don't worry," I said. "I'm not a fan of Jägermeister."

"It's the one...the blonde one...it's her divorce party," the bartender sighed.

"That makes sense," I quipped, before realizing the judgment in my voice.

"What can I get you?"

The bartender did not notice my tone, or care. He was about forty, tan, and in full possession of that relaxed vitality that seemed to swim in the veins of everyone living on the island.

"Just a cup of coffee. Black." I smiled up at him, then looked away to the lights in an empty swimming pool.

In a flash, I was drinking from a cup with the Royal Kona logo on it. The coffee itself was burnt, but the warmth was as soothing as the place that served it. While dialing Nancy, I took a big sip and burned my tongue. When she picked up, I was distracted and couldn't speak right away.

"Sarah? Are you there? Do you know what time it is here?"

Lapsed judgment led me to forget the time difference. It was after midnight, and I had just given her adrenals an uninvited jolt.

"I'm so sorry," I apologized. "I just burnt my tongue, so I couldn't speak right away. I forgot about the time difference."

"Well, what are you doing? Wait, let me go down to the kitchen," she said, starting to perk up a bit.

"I'm at a bar, having a cup of coffee outside by the ocean," I said, my only intent to describe the obvious.

"How romantic. Is Michael there? Tell him I said hello?"

"No, he isn't here. I'm by myself. Not at the resort, actually."

"What? Where are you?"

"In town. Kona. I just felt like going for a drive. I get so cooped up at that resort, Nancy."

"You poor thing." Nancy swung back with sarcasm.

I took another sip of the warm liquid, which had now cooled off and tasted sweeter. I tried to think of what to say next, how much I could tell her.

"Hey, Nancy. Sorry to wake you up," I spoke heavily.

"It's okay, Sarah. Are you sure everything is okay? You seem off or something." Nancy's voice grew concerned.

"How do you know that you're really happy? Like forever happy?"

"Did something happen with Michael?" she said with horror.

"No, nothing like that. I guess I'm just out here by the ocean in the dark getting philosophical."

"You always were the thinker, Sarah. You're fine. Michael loves you."

"But how would you define your happiness, just out of curiosity?"

"Wow, that's a hefty load for the middle of the night. I need a drink for that one. Let's see...the easiest thing to say is that I look forward to each day, each moment of each day. My family is my life. I can't imagine anything different."

I set the phone down for a moment on the bar, holding the mug with both hands. I made eye contact with the bartender, and we smiled at each other. I thought of the women in tight clothes, fishing for youth in an ocean of regret.

"Nancy, I have to go. My battery is about to die. I'll call you tomorrow."

I turned off my phone and ordered another cup of burnt coffee, savoring the taste of the night.

When I returned to my parking space in the familiarity of the morning light, I found no more cat food. The cat had been back to feed. I waited in the car, hoping for it to come looking for another feast. I checked my face in the review mirror and then turned my chin up to scan down my neck. Satisfied with no splotches, I moved the mirror back and looked out again, wondering desperately where the cat might be hiding. Giving up, I stepped out of the car, taking a breath deeper than any I could remember. The air traveled down past my lungs, past my stomach, and into my pelvis. There was a tingling sensation as I exhaled, leaving my face flushed as the breath traveled back up. I remembered the word "radiant" from my wedding day, the incessant use of the word to describe me in my regal dress.

I called out to the cat in earnest many times before resting on the parking strip in the empty lot next to my car. Looking up at the front of the hotel, I already missed the lively streets of Kona. Michael would be awake by now, his eyes filled with crust. His throat would be dry, a morning greeting of parchedness. He'd look over at my side of the bed, whispering to himself words of no consequence. He'd search for a glass of water on the nightstand, pull his hands over his eyes, and let out a small groan. He'd slowly drag himself up to a sitting position, his legs dangling off his side of the bed. Hovering for a bit, he'd consider lying back down before the pain in his head told him otherwise. Hobbling to the bathroom, his temples would sear with pain as he struggled to remember where he'd put the aspirin. After thrashing through drawers, he would finally find the bottle, pour two into his mouth, and then drink them down straight from the sink faucet. Water would splash across his face, the cool feeling both harsh and rewarding. He'd make his way back to bed, call out my name a few times, and then fall back asleep.

Lost in my illustration, the text message coming through caused me to flinch and roll off the parking strip onto the hard cement. It would have been an embarrassing scene, I assume, if I had an audience. Or would I have even noticed? I rolled over to a squatting position and hugged my knees. Jarred but not hurt, I slowly made my way to standing. I had clenched my phone so hard it had become a growth on my hand, the tumor enabling my lust to continue.

The message was from Kalei. *I miss you already. See you on my shift later. Hope you made it back okay. Aloha!*

Chapter 12

~

The magnificence of the next two days was only marred by the blanket of reality I kept having to throw off the bed. Michael returned to his routine of all-day golf while I finally gave purpose to each hour on the clock. I left the hotel whenever I could, sometimes not getting back until after the dinner hour. Michael was relieved that I had found so much to love about Kona—no longer the forlorn wife eating pastries in the room. Kalei arranged his schedule, so he could get off early for the rest of the week, using ideal surfing conditions as an explanation. Despite the impending doom of dealing with the crumpled up blanket of reality, I had never felt more alive and inside myself. At first, it was just my body humming, but the sensations reverberated to every pocket of my being. Suddenly, I was this person, this woman who made decisions and ate cinnamon rolls on the sidewalk.

For our first official date, Kalei took me to a little hut tucked away behind Ali`i Drive for a late afternoon drink. The place, Kanaka Kava, did not serve alcohol but the drink of Hawaiian royalty often known as `awa. Kalei ordered two bowls with a juice mixer to sweeten it up, though it still tasted like dirt. I drank it in three gulps, desperate for a glass of water to wash the taste out. Kalei savored his, a veteran of kava drinking. It wasn't long before my lips went numb, and I started to giggle. The kava had a vaguely narcotic effect, smoothing out the edges as the perfect preamble for an early evening romp. With the time we had left before I had to return to the hotel, we made love for the third and fourth times on Kalei's flimsy mattress.

"I wish you could stay. I want to know what it's like to wake up to you in the morning," he said as I dressed in the kitchen.

"I know," I lamented, not wanting to dwell on it too much.

"What's our plan for tomorrow?" He perked up, his eyes putting my clothes back on the kitchen floor.

"I'll be at Pauahi's bar when you're off. Meet me there, and then we can drive separately into town," I said it with so much control, like I was merely doing business.

I did want to stay there, to go back to bed and never get back out. The kava had just exacerbated the high I had been on since I went to Kalei the night before, actively seeking him.

I had about an hour before I would meet Michael back at our room, but I didn't want to be rushed. I stopped at a coffee shop I had discovered that morning called Lava Java. They served gigantic tear-apart cinnamon rolls and delicious coffee. I sat outside on one of the two-top tables facing Ali'i Drive, pretending my face was one of the pedestrians starting another day of unrelenting brightness.

Michael was already in the room when I returned, reading a paper on the balcony with the news on the TV in the main room. I stuck my head out and cheerfully told him I would get ready quickly. There was no need for small talk. In the privacy of the bathroom, I lingered. I carefully undressed, admiring myself in the mirror, checking for any bite marks. I pulled my hair back, admiring the clarity of my own eyes as though my vision had suddenly been sharpened. In the shower, I had to keep my hands from pleasuring myself as I tried to think of an appropriate restaurant for dinner. In my blissful haze, such practical matters seemed foreign, someone else's business. There was a distance rapidly growing between myself and my own life, and yet it left me more aloof than alarmed.

As I dressed, I called out to Michael to ask him for restaurant suggestions—anything outside of the hotel. He mentioned something called Queen's Marketplace, a high end strip mall just up the road.

"Sounds fine," I shouted, slipping on a pair of heels. I had put on a dress, makeup—my costume contrary of our last date at the bar.

"Wow, you look hot," Michael growled, coming toward me in the bedroom.

I drew away from him, maneuvering to get my second earring in. He flopped on the bed, watching me, a benign mix of tired, horny, and indecisive.

"I think there's a Caribbean place up there," he said with a yawn.

"Great." I crossed through the bedroom and walked briskly toward the front door.

Michael took his time catching up to me, sluggish to commit. He smiled, and it was comfortable. I felt neither dread nor excitement over our dinner together. My travels in the past twenty-four hours had me jet-lagged with joy, in a time zone all to myself.

I volunteered to drive us, as I'd become familiar with the car and local streets. The strip mall was filled with rental cars, beige sedans filled with shopping bags and wet bathing suits. We drove past brightly colored storefronts selling candy, diamonds, the lifestyle we thought we deserved. The Caribbean restaurant was above an Asian-inspired furniture store. Michael asked if I wanted to look around before heading upstairs; I shrugged in apathy, and he took it as a negative.

Stepping from glossy Hawaiian luxury into a boxed version of the Bahamas was seamless. A man named Sal seated us right away and gave us three menus that, in total, rivaled the size of the phone book. I flipped through the drink menu first, undecided between a mojito or something more tropical. Michael ordered his usual beer, the one Kalei drank. I decided to order the same, wondering if it would taste the same as it did in Kalei's apartment.

"Beer?" Michael questioned me.

"Why not?" I was flip as I opened the dinner menu.

"You're really getting into the whole local thing. I love it." Michael leaned forward, hoping to elicit a validation from me. What if I could just tell him he was right? This was the perfect spot for our honeymoon.

After our drinks arrived, we both closed our dinner menus and looked at each other. Michael toasted to "being local," and we took sips of our beers. The taste was slightly floral, not as hoppy as I had remembered. The body seemed lighter as well. I closed my eyes, thinking of Kalei's tongue licking up the bits of foam on top. I wanted to stay there, in the dark, seduced by the chill of the glass. Michael drew me out, though, with another round of questioning.

"So, you're sure you want me to golf every day?"

"I think it's a win-win," I replied, after breaking up with my beer for a moment.

"So what happened? What changed your mind about not wanting to leave?"

The opportunity was there—right there—to tell the truth. It would have been ugly and hurtful, possibly humiliating. But then it would have been out in the open and maybe I would have talked myself out of seeing Kalei the next day. Maybe Michael would have understood, and acquiesced to leaving early. We'd go to marriage counseling, and I'd earn his trust again.

"You were right," I told him, "I was being ungrateful. This is an amazing place."

As the evening went on, an ache for Kalei traveled through my body. When I bit into my shrimp, I wondered if Kalei and I would ever go to a fish market together. When our waiter lit the candle on our table, I saw a red pillar burning next to Kalei's mattress as he kissed my neck. For dessert, I ordered a piece of the famous key lime pie the menu bragged about. It was smooth and silky with a tart bite. I wanted to bake a pie for Kalei. He would be so excited to have something homemade in that little kitchen. I missed his laugh, the way he looked at the ground when he was embarrassed. I missed the muck under his fingernails, the spot on his neck he missed when he was shaving. He tasted like sunflower seeds that had roasted all afternoon in the hot sun, a scorched saltiness I craved. How would I wait until tomorrow to see him again?

We didn't talk on the drive home. After I parked the car, Michael put his hand on my leg and asked if I was okay.

"I'm fine," I smiled back, continuing to open the car door.

Michael hesitated and then opened the passenger door, cautiously letting himself onto the parking lot. I surveyed the area quickly for the cat, not wanting Michael to notice. If I had seen it, I would have scooped it up and never let it go. We could drive away together. I'd give it a name, a life, nice things.

I felt like walking just as much as I wanted to avoid being in that room with Michael. We strolled through the lobby and out past the pool and then headed down to the beach. We didn't go down the trail like I had done in the early days of our honeymoon. I thought back to that day, a confused woman desperate for an epiphany, unaware of her extremities. A thin layer of darkness hovered before the entrance to the trail, a barrier stopping us. Beyond the safety of the resort's tiki torches, a vague sense of endangerment overcame me. If Michael disappeared, I thought, I'd just keep walking down to the beach. Maybe I'd dip a foot in the dark ocean, summoning a cold rush of thrilling anxiety.

"Should we head back?" Michael asked.

"It's getting chilly." I turned around and started walking back to the room.

Back in the room, I complained about being cold with no specific plea. Michael lay down on the bed and turned on the television, kicking off his shoes and letting out a deep sigh. I went to the bathroom and started filling the tub with hot water, setting my bag down next to it.

"Taking a bath?" Michael yelled from the bed.

"Something to warm me up." I came back out to respond, leaving the water running.

"You sure you're okay?" he asked again, this time more curious.

"Just cold," I mumbled, and smiled at him, looking forward to shutting everything out.

With the door shut and locked, I reached my phone out of my bag and immediately sent Kalei a text message: *About to take a bath. Wish you were here.*

I began to undress, catching my own smirk in the mirror. When the last piece of clothing hit the bathroom floor, a draft flew through the room. I hurried to the tub, phone in right hand, eagerly anticipating a dirty response.

You wouldn't get very clean with me there. Aloha!

The innuendo intensified with each message sent back and forth, culminating in text message intercourse. I covered my mouth to avoid making noise, but, beyond that discretion, I had transported myself without much concern or awareness of my surroundings. We texted goodnight, and I continued to soak, warm in the wet cocoon I created.

Michael surprised me the next morning with a room service cart topped with plates of bacon, eggs, waffles, and plumeria blossoms. He crawled back into bed with me, cozying up to my side and pouring us each a cup of coffee. It was the first time I truly felt the hot sting of remorse, a rubber band snapping against my bare flesh. It was worse than regret, as if it had only been a momentary lapse in judgment. I sat in bed, trying to assuage myself, so the morning could be pleasant. A part of me missed splashing around in the pleasant puddles with Michael back home. There had never been a deep end to worry about.

"What's on your agenda today?" Michael asked me with a mouthful of scrambled eggs.

"I think I'll drive around?" I asked myself, setting down my cup of coffee on the nightstand.

"Anywhere in particular?"

"Might go shopping in town." I started to speak with my mouth hovering over a piece of waffle I had just torn off.

"Be careful."

I merely nodded, thinking about the box of condoms at Kalei's apartment. My stomach turned, and I was unable to eat more than a few bites. Still, I wanted to stay and honor Michael's sweet gesture. I rested my head on his shoulder, thanking him. He kissed my head, and I closed my eyes; the snapping returned, quietly painful.

As soon as Michael began to get ready, I readied to escape the room. I splashed water on my face, rinsed with mouthwash, pulled my hair back and changed into a yellow dress that was crumpled in the bottom drawer of the dresser. I didn't even look in the mirror before pecking Michael on the lips and scooping the essentials into my bag.

Ali'i Drive was quiet when I arrived that morning, a few older couples heading into the ABC Store for souvenirs. I stopped in to buy a notebook, a journal to bind my racing thoughts. I became distracted by the colorful beach towels near the front of the store, holding several up as I used to do with sweaters in department stores. The buzzing of my phone drew me away. It was Nancy. *How are you? Haven't heard from you. Everything okay? Worried.* I threw the phone back into my bag and wandered over to a display of tropical-themed snow globes. One of them had a Santa figurine riding a dolphin. It made me smile, so I picked it up. I shook and shook, enthralled by the glittery snow drifting down against Santa's white beard. I held onto it as I perused the notebooks in the next aisle. They all had pictures of whales or turtles or beach scenes, some larger than others. I settled on one with a school of tropical fish on the cover. They were swimming away from frenetic tourists, toward peace.

"Just one snow globe and one journal?" the cashier asked with mild disappointment.

"Yes, thanks." I tried not to make eye contact with her.

After ringing me up, she reminded me to save my receipts for a gift redemption. She was so earnest about it, dedicated to the value of a free mug or beach towel. I tucked the receipt inside my wallet and walked north on Ali'i Drive, past a ratty group of teenagers waiting for the bus. Locals were easy to spot in a tourist town, moving and waiting without the freedom and tan lines. I climbed a few steps as the sidewalk moved further away from the street. I glanced into the windows of an art gallery, fixing sharply on a gorgeous oil on canvas of the cardinal I had spotted at the resort. I looked up at the name of the gallery—Ma'ikai—and then wandered in. I walked right up to the bird painting, admiring its realism.

"Beautiful, isn't it?"

A man came and stood next to me, wearing a black and white aloha shirt tucked into crisp black slacks. He had a name tag that read "Kevin, Assistant Manager."

"Yes, I spotted it from outside and just had to come see it up close. I love those birds," I said, looking back at the painting.

"Where are you from?" he asked, as all the service people did.

"San Francisco."

"I love that city! I lived there in my early twenties. Crazy times," he laughed, revealing a set of wrinkles around his eyes. He appeared to be in his early forties, just a decade ahead of me.

"It's a nice place to live." I looked at him, warming to his gregarious demeanor.

"What brings you to Kona?"

I hesitated, remembering I had tucked my wedding ring away in my bag on the drive over. "I'm visiting my boyfriend. He lives here."

"Long distance relationship? Been there. I met the man of my dreams one weekend in San Diego. Turns out, not so much the man of my dreams. Sorry, that was rude."

"No, it's fine. Honesty is refreshing. My boyfriend is younger, very attractive," I said, happy to know he was gay. I missed my gay friends. Somehow, they all disappeared between graduation and quitting work.

"What's it like here, you know, meeting other men?" I decided to pry, feeling inspired by his transparency.

"Not that bad, I don't think. Although, I'm married, so it's been a long time since I've really tried." He held up his left hand to reveal a simple titanium ring.

"Did you meet here?" I asked, now fully disengaged from the painting.

"Yes. Actually, he owns a bar down the street. About ten years ago, he bought a painting from me. And there you have it," he laughed, this time seeming a bit more exposed.

"That's romantic," I said, before changing the subject. "How much is this bird one?"

"That one is twenty-seven hundred, but I can give you a discount if you want to frame it yourself back in San Francisco," Kevin said, casually rehearsed.

"I think that's a bit too much for me right now. It's really lovely, though. This whole gallery." I took a turn to look at the other side, eyeing volcanoes, sunsets, wood sculptures, and stunning photographs of bamboo.

"Well, here's my card in case you come into a windfall. What does your boyfriend do?"

"He works at a hotel," I said. "One of the nice ones up the coast."

"Very nice. Do you get a discount?" he laughed, a gleam in his eye.

"Something like that," I responded, starting to flush from the lying.

"Well, enjoy your trip. My name is Kevin, as you can see. What was yours?"

"Sarah."

"Well, Sarah, you have very good taste. Have you ever worked in a gallery?"

"No, but I used to work with artists. I studied art history," I downplayed.

"Hey, you should have my job." Kevin mocked himself and smiled widely.

I tucked his business card away in my bag and wandered around the gallery while Kevin moved on to a new customer who had just entered. On my way out, I made a point to interrupt him to say goodbye. I wished I could have sat down with him for an afternoon, asking him questions and learning about his life.

"Aloha," he called out to me as my feet landed on the sidewalk in front of the gallery.

I turned and waved back to him, envious of the customer who now had his full attention.

My phone rang again. And again. Still Nancy. I kept ignoring her, setting out to find a place to start my journal. The new journal.

As soon as Pauahi saw me walk into the Pu'uhonua lounge, she assiduously began mixing my margarita. A slight smile came over her face as I took a seat at the bar. We exchanged our "alohas" and she set down my usual drink order. Her face was softer now, like that stern school teacher who finally warms up the day before winter break when kids bring her presents. I reached into my bag for my journal, noticing the snow globe I had purchased in my moment of whimsy. I set the globe on the bar, wondering what kind of reaction it might draw from Pauahi. She said nothing until I pulled out my journal.

"*Humu*," she muttered.

"Excuse me?" I asked.

"The fish on your book. It's the state fish. Humu."

I looked down at the fish, the reason I had chosen that particular journal. The fish were a pale brown with black streaks across the middle. They wore bright yellow lipstick, a contrast to their stoic demeanor.

"Actually, the real name is *Humuhumu nuku apua'a*. But I don't expect you to say all that," Pauahi laughed, then looked at my snow globe with a hint of judgment before walking away. All of the glitter had settled to the bottom now, revealing the faded red of Santa's hat.

I sat with my margarita, my journal, and my snow globe with the excitement of seeing Kalei at any moment. I looked back at what I had written earlier at the cafe, disappointed by its insignificance. The first page was a drawing of three stick figures on a beach with a giant escalator rising up from the ocean. I crossed out two of the stick figures, disgusted at my drawing, and closed the journal. I shook the snow globe again, marveling at it while I finished my drink. Pauahi was at the other end of the bar helping a young woman who had just sat down. When she came back to fix her cocktail, she stopped to ask if I was okay.

"I'm good," I said, fumbling with the journal.

"Okay," she said. The concern on her face made me realize she wasn't asking if I needed another drink.

I had turned off the vibrate function on my phone to avoid Nancy even further, but needed to check for any messages from Kalei. This time, there was only one text from my older sister: *I take this to mean you're having fun, so I'll stop bugging you. Just let me know you didn't get eaten by a shark or something. Love ya!* I smiled in relief and tossed the phone back in my bag. Pauahi was fixing something complicated for the new customer, involving several shots of rum and a back scratcher. The woman's face lit up when Pauahi set it down in front of her. She took a picture with her phone, and then took a large sip, bumping her nose against the back scratcher. I laughed a little to myself, not so much that anyone noticed, and then looked at Pauahi to see if she saw the same thing. She had returned to counting bottles, though, so I returned to my snow globe.

When Kalei snuck up behind me and grabbed my shoulders, I immediately knew it was him. I wanted nothing more than to indulge in a shoulder rub, but I quickly turned on the discretion by turning around in my seat.

"Hey there," I said, looking at his toothy grin.

"Aloha," he said, somehow still grinning while he talked. "Sorry I'm late. I actually have to go back in a bit to sign for some snorkel cruise tickets for some guests, but I wanted to see you as soon as I could. Let's have a drink."

Kalei took the seat next to me and waved at Pauahi, who had just turned around. She looked at us both in a knowing and calm manner. A measured pour later, Kalei had his pint of lager on a coaster with the hotel's logo and the word "relax" on it.

"What's up, Pauahi?" Kalei asked rather loudly after taking his first sip.

"Not much. You change your shift?" she asked, staring at his chest.

"Yeah, been getting off earlier. I showed Sarah here the whole island the other day. She even swam at Ahalanui. She's afraid of the water," Kalei laughed, leaving me slightly derided.

I looked at Kalei for a prompt. How should we act in front of her? I wanted to hold hands, to kiss him on the cheek. His looseness about our affection made me all the more tense.

"Good for you," Pauahi said before moving on to a new customer standing at the other end of the bar asking about drink specials.

I leaned in closer to Kalei without conveying too much intimacy. I touched his knee under the bar, and he grabbed my hand. He was already turned on, I could tell.

"Do you think she knows?" I whispered to him.

"Pauahi? No, I don't think so. She's kind of an old soul, though," Kalei stage-whispered back.

Pauahi had not asked me if I wanted another drink. I glanced at Kalei's now half-empty beer, then shifted my gaze toward my half-full glass.

"Hey, what's with the snow globe?" Kalei finally made the observation.

I picked it up and shook it in front of his face until he let out a goofy laugh, reminding me of the sounds boys would make in gym class when one of their peers fell down.

"Just something I picked up at the ABC Store, along with my journal here," I said, putting the snow globe back down on the bar.

Kalei grabbed the journal and held it up high, taunting me like an older brother who'd just gotten a hold of an embarrassing love letter.

"Give it back," I whispered emphatically.

"What are you writing about, Sarah?" he asked, still holding it up.

I reached up and grabbed it from him, almost losing my balance and falling off my bar stool. He looked shocked, and immediately shut down. He turned his body toward the bar and took a long, meditative sip of his beer.

"I'm sorry," I said, and then turned to slurp from my drink.

"I get it," he said. "It's private."

He really was sorry. It made me wonder if I was being too private, if I should let him in more. Maybe I had never taken my hand off the emergency break these past few days with him. It was my ninth day on the island. My flight would leave in five days. Five days was all we had in which to cultivate anything resembling a relationship.

"How much time we got before your husband gets back?" Kalei asked, a twinkle in his eye.

I hated hearing the word *husband*. I hated it so much that I had to wave Pauahi over for a refill on my margarita. I sat in silence, almost pouting, bubbling with frustration. Pauahi rapidly returned with my cocktail. I drank, retreating into myself, staring at the television above the bar. The news was on, and they were showing footage of a storm somewhere in the Midwest. A tornado had ravaged an entire community. A woman's whole life had been impossibly spread across a field. What would she miss most?

"Are you okay?" Kalei finally broke the silence.

I turned around to face him again. "I'm fine. I just don't like hearing the word 'husband' when I'm with you," I whispered.

"I get it. So do we have time for a rendezvous?" he asked.

I looked at the clock above the bar and tried calculating Michael's timing with driving time back to Kalei's apartment. It was tight, and having him in my hotel room would just take my adultery to a level I wasn't ready to confront. As much as I wanted him physically, there was a surprising satisfaction to just sitting together in public.

"Can we just sit here?" I asked.

"Sure," he said back without any disappointment.

We took sips of our drinks while looking at each other with eyes of infatuation. Serenity swept over me; I wanted to hold hands but nothing more. We did so under the bar for a few moments, absorbing each other. Kalei would say we were connecting our *mana*, our life force. As I admired this man before me, whom I really barely knew, I tried to picture a life where this was normal. What happened when the—I hated to think it—the honeymoon period was over and we settled into a routine? Would I have dinner ready when Kalei got off his shift? Would we live in that little apartment? As our connection blossomed beyond orgasms, for the first time I could see beyond the next five days.

"What do you want with me?" I asked, watching his face drop as if I'd just told him I was pregnant. He looked at his watch, then ran his fingers through his hair. He hadn't shaved in a few days; I tried to imagine him with a full beard and mustache.

"I should go sign those papers. I'll be back in about fifteen," he said as he scooted off his stool. He, then, leaned over and whispered into my ear, "I want you all to myself."

Joy must have emanated from my face; Pauahi gave me a strange, questioning look. She came toward me, strict and cool.

"Another margarita?" she asked in a curt tone.

"Oh, no! I should wait," I said, "Kalei is coming back after he finishes some paperwork at the desk."

And then things got weird. Pauahi leaned down against the bar, her body more casual but her face tense and concentrated. She knew everything. I wanted to sign for my drinks and run away. I wished I could vanish into my snow globe, a life of glitter and year-round Christmas. Sooner or later, she would say something, and it wouldn't be pleasant.

"How long have you been on this island?" she asked in a softer voice than usual.

"About ten days," I said. "It's a two week vacation."

"Right, a vacation," she said, emphasizing my temporary status.

I didn't say anything, not sure why she was getting involved. She and Kalei were close. Maybe she wanted to scare me away from her surrogate son. Or maybe she just didn't like me. I thought the latter was most likely as our interactions seemed so tepid.

"He's just a boy," she finally said.

I looked down in shame, biting my lip and searching for the right words to defend myself. I had taken advantage of him, she thought.

"I know. I care about him, Pauahi," I said with as much directness as I could muster.

"You don't know him," she said. "Men that age, their brains aren't fully formed yet. He thinks he knows, but he's here to find himself. He's just on a longer vacation than you."

"You think I'm going to hurt him?" I asked in my most incredulous tone.

"No. I'm looking out for you. We *wahine* need to have each other's backs."

I was pleasantly surprised by Pauahi's apparent concern for my happiness, but there was a lack of heart in her voice. Instead of feeling the warm embrace of an older woman's friendship, I just felt judged.

"I appreciate it, Pauahi, but I can take care of myself," I said, folding my arms.

Pauahi pushed herself back up, standing erect and rigid over the bar. Her face was visibly disappointed, but the strength in her body compensated.

"You know what you want, then," she said, plainly, and then walked away to help other customers.

I squeezed my folded arms against my body, consoling myself with my own hug. Fighting back tears of anger, I directed my rage at the stupid snow globe. I unfolded my arms and grabbed it with my right hand, squeezing it and then throwing it violently into my bag. I hoped it would break, not thinking of the practicality of a bag full of liquid glitter. I wanted to flee, but pride kept me seated right there where I would welcome my boy lover on vacation in just a few minutes. However, my exchange with Pauahi would leave an indelible imprint. I wanted to hate her, to ignore all that she said, the bitter old bartender. She didn't know me. Had she ever been to San Francisco and met my family? Had she ever met Michael? The worst part of it all was that somehow she knew I didn't really know what I wanted and still said those words. I had been so full of life just as Kalei told me he wanted me to himself, the first glimpse into a future. Sure, I was on vacation. But Kalei belonged here. The island had become part of his DNA. He was local. I thought about what vacation meant, thinking about the past several years of my life and a future with Michael. When would I not be on vacation?

Chapter 13

I didn't sleep a minute that night, poring over the image of Pauahi's face, hearing her voice with every toss and turn. I finally moved to the next room and sat down at a writing desk next to the television. I brought my journal with me, intending to figure out what I wanted, as Pauahi seemed to suggest at the bar. There was an oval mirror above the desk. I watched myself just sitting there, idly at the desk, waiting for something to happen.

Michael slept soundly in the bedroom; he'd had several Sapporos at dinner. We tried out the hotel's sushi restaurant, which Michael adored. He ate most of our order while I spent the entire meal trying to self-talk my stomach into submission.

Kalei's paperwork turned into a short meeting, so we only had a few minutes to talk when he returned. I wanted to talk to him about Pauahi and ask him if he was on the island for life, but there was not sufficient time to dig into such depth before departing. He'd text me the next day, and we'd make plans again, hopefully some private time to talk about the future.

I turned the page in my journal and wrote two names on the top: *Michael, Kalei*. I underlined each one and then drew a vertical line down the middle to create two columns. Next, I started writing down words, any I could associate with each name. I must have spent an hour diligently crafting these two columns. When I felt I could not summon one more single letter, I closed the journal and stared into the mirror. I looked tired: not just sleep deprived, but a kind of tired that comes from living within oneself for too long. I closed my eyes, but it did nothing to ameliorate my anxiety.

The clock turned over to five o'clock. The night had always been my most difficult time. I just knew if I could make it to sunlight, then I could distract myself. There would be chores to do, coffee to drink, people to meet. I hated those moments in the dark because they made me second guess, from something as trivial as a dress I'd purchased earlier in the week to the wording on a thank-you card to Michael's mother, to not taking more math classes in college. I continued staring into the mirror, wondering if my face would eventually start to resemble Michael's. Opening my journal back up, I began to carefully review each word I had written down as though I were making the final perusal of my dissertation. Each word needed to attach firmly to the name, so they became interrelated.

When I was eight, my dad put in a new walkway to the front of our house. After the cement was poured, Nancy and I got to put our hands in the goop before it dried. It was cold and sticky, but we were thrilled to get our hands dirty.

"Now you'll always be here," my father said as we watched our paw prints dry. It was a pure moment, one that I didn't appreciate until years later when I started to become disappointed in the people around me—particularly boys. I'd open the front door and there I was, right where I belonged with people who loved me. My two lists should have given me a logical answer, but, once I really started seeing the names and the words underneath each one, I realized I had already made my decision before writing a single word.

At seven o'clock, I slipped back into the bedroom, in stealth mode so as not to awaken Michael. He'd be asleep for another hour, at least, so I had time to shower and dress in the stillness of the early morning. I didn't pay much attention to him when I tiptoed to the bathroom, as I focused steadily on each step to take to enact my plan. I took a medium length shower, neither indulgent nor abbreviated. I washed until my body felt clean, not bothering with my hair. I'd pin it back in some pragmatic-but-still-feminine look. After I dried off, I wrapped myself in a bath towel and began to wash my face. There were days when my morning routine could be languorous, but this would be simply systematic. I moisturized appropriately, brushed my teeth, filed my finger nails, cleaned my ears, applied light foundation and lip gloss to achieve an air of femininity, and rolled my stick of deodorant under each arm. I pulled my hair back and studied myself in the bathroom mirror just briefly, not wanting to sidestep into a monotony of musings. I slunk out of the bathroom, opening the dresser as slowly as possible, and pulled out a pair of white walking shorts, clean underwear, and a blue cotton T-shirt with bejeweled birds across the breast. Back inside the bedroom, I found my bra and began to dress for the day. When finished, I decided to make coffee in the other room with the in-room coffee maker I had yet to turn on. By the time Michael woke up, I would be freshly composed, alert, and new.

At ten minutes past eight o'clock, the bedroom door opened, and Michael shuffled out. He was wearing only his boxers, a red pair with basketballs on them, which I had given to him as a gift on his last birthday. His arms had become browner, but the rest of his torso remained pale. His nose was peeling; his dried skin probably littered the bed. I sat at the writing desk with my first cup of coffee, considering each sip as a measure of the finite time I had until the conversation.

"I've never noticed this desk before," he said.

"It's nice," I responded.

Michael looked down at my cup and then around the room, searching for the elusive room service cart. I watched him, perplexed by the apparition of a breakfast beverage, realizing that he hadn't noticed other parts of the room as well.

"I made a pot. There's a coffeemaker over there," I said, and pointed to the small appliance in the corner of the room.

Michael's confusion morphed into pleasant surprise as he tentatively made his way across the room to pour himself a cup.

"Look at that," he mumbled to himself.

There was nondairy creamer, all kinds of sweeteners, and even stir sticks! After a taste test, Michael retired to the sofa. If I sat in my chair facing the mirror in front of me, I could see him perfectly. Still, at some point, I would need to turn around to really address him. A few more sips, I decided. We both needed a bit more time. Once the caffeine kicked in, Michael's morning chatterbox personality emerged.

"So, that sushi place was tremendous. Didn't you think? Sorry you weren't all that hungry. We'll have to go back. God, I can't believe we only have a few more days. I seriously want to extend. I was talking to a guy yesterday who just bought a condo in South Kona."

He continued like that for several minutes, yammering on about the sun helping productivity and wanting to come back for Thanksgiving. Nothing he said was unusual or surprising until after he took a short pause. He leaned forward on the sofa, setting his cup of coffee on the table in front of him. Both of his hands came together into a prayer position and then brushed up against his face. I knew something serious was coming. I turned around.

"Sarah, I need to ask you something. It's...I'm...I..."

My temples tensed up, twisting the ball of yarn inside my head into a tight knot.

"What's wrong?" I asked, putting him out of his stammering misery.

"Did you sleep at all last night? I woke up a few times, and you weren't there."

The yarn loosened a little, and I let out an audible sigh.

"I didn't sleep at all. Sorry if I worried you. I tried not to wake you," I said, trying not to sound overly relieved.

"It's okay. That's actually not what I wanted to ask you. Sarah, is there something going on with you that I should know about?"

It felt like my head was trying to detach itself from my body. My moment at the guillotine had finally arrived. Michael's face was diminished, expressions of a time before he held any power. Time marched on, waiting for me. But this wasn't part of the plan. Suddenly powerless, my actions could only be reactionary.

"There is something. But let's talk about it later. It's nothing to worry about, though," I said.

He covered his face with both hands and sunk back into the sofa. A dark cloud of concern hung low in the room. I switched back and forth between watching Michael in the mirror and gazing upon my own reflection. Neither brought any sense of peace. I finished my cup of coffee. Michael left his cup on the table, slouching even lower in the sofa. I looked down at the desk, noticing the fine details in the daylight. There was a thin border of etching on all four sides, resembling some type of petroglyph. The craftsmanship of the wood casing around the mirror was stunning. As I was about to break the silence, Michael sprung up like a toy whose battery had only been momentarily shut down. He smiled, even beamed a little bit and then walked toward me. He put his hands on my shoulders, giving me a gentle massage. Given how tense I was, his touch felt nice.

"I'll just play nine holes today, so we have more time to talk," he said.

All I could think of was my day with Kalei. Would we still have time to make it back to his apartment and make love? I really needed for him to hold me, assure me, blanket me with affirmation. Michael removed his hands from my shoulders and leaned down to kiss the back of my head. I gave him a smile through the mirror.

"I'm going to get ready. In the mood for breakfast today?"

"Still not feeling well," I said.

Instinct told Michael not to push on the subject; all would be revealed soon enough. He disappeared into the bedroom, and, shortly after, I could hear the shower running. He'd get ready for his day, pick up something to eat, and then enjoy a half day of golf with his new friends. It would be a sunny day, probably reach eighty-four degrees. The cardinals would be out, and occasionally land on the impossibly green golf course. One of those mongooses might show up. Michael would have a good day, I told myself. He'd get to eat whatever he wanted for breakfast and lunch and probably enjoy a few beers on the course. He would feel the occasional breeze brush up against his polo shirt, keeping him from perspiring too much. His friends would tell funny jokes about their wives. Michael would laugh, but not respond. All day long there would be a pit in his stomach, but he'd ignore it and remind himself not to worry. "She loves me," he'd say to himself.

As soon as Michael shut the door, I got up from the desk and began pacing the room. My plan needed to be altered, but not by much. I turned the coffee maker off and sent Kalei a short text: *Michael just left. Be down to the desk in a few.* I thought of what I might need, but had no clear picture of how I'd spend the day. I put my phone, wallet and journal in my bag and left the room, considering whether or not I would see it differently when I returned later in the day.

Inside the elevator, I became aflutter with anticipation of seeing Kalei. It would be different this time. I'd smile knowingly at him. I was all his now. I tucked my wedding ring in the left pocket of my shorts just before the doors opened to the lobby. Around the corner, I would see my man. I practiced my smile a few times, predicting the look on Kalei's face. I clasped my hands together and turned the corner; the concierge desk would now be in full view. And there he was not. Standing behind the desk was a young woman, maybe twenty-five, blond hair cut short and severe. Her face was pretty enough, but there was an intensity to her—pursed lips, heavy eyeliner, too many rings on her fingers. Her uniform was different than Kalei's, and when I looked across the lobby at the reservations desk, I noticed she wore the same uniform as the women there. Did she get promoted overnight? I rushed over to the desk and immediately asked about Kalei.

"He doesn't work here anymore." The woman gave her terse response.

"What?" I asked. My voice had a hostile tone that I never knew existed.

"I'm filling in for the day. I usually work over at the reservations desk," she responded without conviction.

My mind raced. I had to follow up. What was going on?

"What do you mean? He worked here yesterday. Just yesterday afternoon he had to fill out paperwork," I said.

"I don't know much. Sorry. And we're not allowed to say whether he was fired or resigned. Company policy," Kalei's replacement said.

"Well, it's really important I talk to him!" I shouted.

The girl looked stunned, the intensity on her face softened or maybe bullied into submission by my force. Could I have been the reason Kalei was fired? I looked at the girl's name tag. Her name was Susan.

"I'm sorry, Susan," I pleaded. "It's just that Kalei is a friend of mine. I'm just so surprised he didn't tell me that he is no longer employed here."

Susan's face grew intense again, her wheels cranking at full speed. She looked at me as if noticing me for the first time.

"Wait. Are you Sarah?" she asked.

"Yes. Why?"

Susan reached underneath the desk and pulled out a white business-sized envelope. I could see my name written on it. I felt a sense of panic. Was Kalei dead? Did he drown?

"Kalei wanted you to have this. He told his supervisor to make sure you got this letter," Susan said and handed me the envelope.

"Is he okay?" I asked, but, really, I meant to say, "If he's okay, just tell me."

"I think so. He's not dead or anything if that's what you mean," Susan said, starting to become annoyed at my persistence. I thanked her for the letter and turned around, unsure of where to go read it. Why was he leaving me notes? Why wouldn't he call or text? I pulled my phone out of my bag. He had not returned my text yet, which was very out of character. He was always so responsive. I looked around for a bench or a chair, but there were so many people in the lobby. I wandered out-side to the front of the resort, where people were pulling up in their rental cars to unload their baggage. To my left there was a small wooden bench, tucked far enough away to seem quasi-private. I ran to the bench and collapsed into it. The hard surface hurt my butt, but I shook it off. I held the envelope in both hands, staring at the letters that made up my name. It was definitely Kalei's handwriting; I recognized it from the letter he left at my door when he told me to meet him at his apartment. After conjecturing the content inside the envelope from benign (he has to leave town for a sick relative but will be back soon) to the horrific (he's in love with someone else or doesn't think I'm good enough), I ripped off the band aid and began reading. The letter was handwritten, on the hotel's stationary.

Sarah,

First off, I want to apologize for not being man enough to do this in person. Part of it is being afraid and part of it is timing. By the time you read this, I will either be on a plane or on my way to the airport. Yesterday, when I left you to sign some papers, I was not completely honest. I had to call someone back, my agent from New York. She had been calling me all week, and, that morning, I finally called her back. She has a part for me, a big one, on a soap opera. I know it sounds cheesy, but it's a really great opportunity for me to get back in the game. Last night, I thought about it, and thought about it, and realize how much I miss acting and being in New York. It's kind of like the past two years have been this extended vacation for me. And you have helped me realize that, Sarah. You are an amazing woman, and I feel so blessed to know you and to have been intimate with you. I know it wasn't a long time, but I felt like we had a pretty intense connection. I hope you feel that way, too. But also, you should forget about me and get back to your amazing life in San Francisco. We needed each other, Sarah. This place lets you be who you want to be, and I love that. But it's time now for me to go back to being Scott in New York, the real me. And you get to be Mrs. Chizeck. You will have an awesome life; I just know it. I'm sorry if this hurts you, or if I misled you in any way. Sometimes, maybe we just need to get away from our own reality to realize why we belong there in the first place. I was afraid to fail in New York, so I fled, and the island gave me an opportunity to go somewhere else with my identity. I changed my name, my interests, the way I talked, everything. But was it just a new kind of acting challenge, testing me to see how well I could adapt and authenticate this new character? I'm not totally sure, and I genuinely love Hawaiʻi and her people. I hope I didn't screw things up for you and Michael. In the end, I think he's the right guy for you. He always was. Take care, Sarah. It's probably best we don't keep in touch, but I'll always remember the special time we shared.

Aloha,

Scott, aka Kalei

I read the letter two more times, then crumpled it up into a ball, unfolded it and read it a fourth time. I, then, placed the letter back in its envelope and tucked it neatly into my bag. I looked toward the hotel entrance, spotting a family of four arriving for a fun-filled vacation. A boy, around nine years old, already wore an aloha shirt while his sister wore a baseball cap with all eight of the Hawaiian islands in bright pink.

I wanted to weep but felt stunned and exposed. I kept thinking of what was missing in the letter. Just yesterday he told me he wanted me all to himself, and yet he never addressed it. Was he acting? If he knew he was going to call his agent, had he already made up his mind? Was he just telling me what I wanted to hear? When did he actually write the letter?

I pulled out my phone to call Kalei and demand answers, but something stopped me. I wasn't sure what, exactly, but I was not compelled to dial his number. I slowly rose from the bench and began walking in no particular direction, away from the hotel. Once I was twenty feet or so from the lobby entrance, the tears trickled down my face. It was an odd sensation because I hadn't even realized I was crying until I felt the warm sting against my cheek. I needed a place to release; I walked toward the rental car. When I shut the driver's seat door, a seal formed, and all the energy and motion outside of the car became muted and slow. I pulled the letter out and read it for the fifth time. Sobbing, I rested my head against the steering wheel, imagining a soft pillow next to a purring cat that would lull me to sleep. Remembering the stray cat,

I shot up and looked through the car windows, hoping to spot it, so I could scoop it up and hold it for hours. I opened the car door and looked underneath the car and then behind it. Defeated, I crawled back into the driver's seat and slammed the door shut. I continued to sob for several minutes until a point where the hysterical crying morphed into hysterical laughter. What a mess, I thought about myself. How could anyone end up here? A dark and violent anger came over me, spurring me to act in some capacity. I dug the car keys out of my bag, which I had placed on the passenger seat, and started the ignition. I knew where I needed to go.

The island's Costco was up from the Kona shore, toward the mountains, what Kalei used to call *mauka*. The inside looked just like the one on Tenth Street back home aside from a showcasing of Spam near the main entrance. I thought I would have the place to myself Saturday afternoon. Michael and I didn't frequent the Costco in San Francisco very often. In fact, I can't remember the two of us ever there together. I had probably made five or six trips, usually right before hosting a party or when I happened to be in the neighborhood. I once bought a set of sheets there and then never took them out of the package. I thought they would come in handy as an extra set.

I walked past the cash registers and food court and then stopped, taking in the fast-paced normalcy. Even on a tropical island, people needed bulk toilet paper and giant bags of mini quiches. The familiarity startled me, and I began to shuffle back and forth, moving just a few inches to the left and then to the right. I must have looked helpless, mentally off-kilter. Behind me the voice of a boy twisted me around.

"Can I help you?" he asked with a hint of fear.

"I'm looking for the cat food," I replied, as if it were the most normal thing.

"Aisle ten, just right down there." He pointed toward a display of red vines in large plastic jars.

"Thank you," I said and walked away.

When I got to aisle ten, I was overwhelmed by both the variety of cat food and size of bags. Having never owned a cat, I had no idea which brands were healthy. I supposed for a stray cat, any food would be healthier than none. I spotted the smallest bag I could find, something called Chef's Blend, and picked it up. My face turned hot from the physical exertion it took to hold onto the bag. Biting my lip, I walked as quickly as I could toward the cash register without dropping the cat food. Once I made it to the red vine display, I put the bag down for a rest. It was then that the distraction wore off, and my mind drifted back to Kalei's letter. It was a problem I needed to solve, or, at least, have explained to me. I thought of him on a two-year extended vacation, returning to Manhattan a sun-kissed superstar. And then just as I was about to pick up the cat food for the final stretch, I realized my resolve: *Pauahi*. She made this happen. Emboldened by a rush of rage, I carried the hefty bag of cat food to the register without breaking a sweat. My focus narrowed steadily until it was a laser pointing directly behind that bar, at that smug woman serving margaritas.

I shoved the bag of cat food into the backseat, realizing I had not yet turned to sugar to ameliorate what I was feeling. It hadn't even occurred to me to pick up a box of candy or a tub of licorice. I moved the car from one parking lot to another; there appeared to be some sort of construction on the highway causing delays. I sat and waited, and waited, watching the frustration of the man behind me in my rearview mirror. His face was naturally red, but it was the way he scrunched up his nose that gave his mood away. After a solid fifteen minutes, I was able to inch forward a few feet. This continued for over an hour. I turned the radio on and off, switched stations, fiddled with the air conditioning, gazed out the driver's seat window, and occasionally checked my phone for messages. The terrible traffic confused me; I felt displaced by the bustle of Costco shoppers and frustrated commuters. The car's gas tank was dangerously close to empty. I wanted to cry again, but there were no tears left.

Finally clearing the construction site some ninety minutes later, I slammed my foot on the accelerator and rolled down all the windows. Speeding would have been fun, were it not for my current situation. Rather, I was only trying to get somewhere unpleasant faster. I had to slam on the breaks when I got to the hotel parking lot, having not paid attention to my speed. I turned sharply into my parking spot and abruptly turned off the engine before manically pulling up the emergency break. I got out of the car and opened up the back seat door to access the bag of cat food. Ripping the top, I slid the bag close to the door and just let the food trickle down into a small mound next to the car. After giving a quick look for the cat, I got back in the driver's seat to wait. The car was hot, and I started to feel sticky. I took Kalei's letter out again and read it slowly, hanging on to each word and punctuation mark. Trying to avoid my compulsion with the letter, I shoved it into the glove compartment. I wanted to call Nancy, tell her everything and hear her comforting voice. Would she understand? She'd be offended, I thought. My actions were an affront to her very existence. Still, I longed for her friendship. A profound sorrow overcame me, replacing the anger momentarily. I pictured Nancy's face with its angles of perpetual hope as she watched me open her wedding gift. The picture worsened my mood, so I opened the glove compartment and read the letter again, again capturing the vehemence necessary to move forward. I sat and waited until it was close to noon. The cat never appeared.

I trampled through tranquility with fury and focus, holding firmly the vivid image of Pauahi's proud mouth. The bar wasn't open yet, but I could not wait a second longer to confront the woman who thwarted my carefully thought-out plan. Like a sniper's bullet, I arrived suddenly, ready to penetrate my target. Her face looked the same as when I first met her: tight, judgmental, stoic. She spoke before I could land my first hit.

"I'm not open yet," she said, trying to stare me into submission.

"I know. I need to talk to you. What did you say to Kalei?" I yelled.

"I don't know what you're talking about. I haven't seen Kalei since the two of you were here yesterday."

I wanted her face to read deceit, but it unfortunately did not. Was she this good? She *had* to be the reason Kalei left.

"Really?" I said in my most mocking tone. "So you didn't happen to mention any of that vacation crap to him? Because it's all over his letter."

"What letter?" she asked, seeming genuine in her confusion.

I pulled the letter out of my bag, like a lucky card I'd been holding for an entire game. I didn't wish for her to read it; it was a prop that enabled my drama.

"This letter! He left it for me at the concierge desk. He's leaving. He left. Why? I don't understand. He said he needed to be back in New York. What did he say to you?" I begged.

"Kalei left? I see now. No, I had no idea. Like I said, I didn't see him after the two of you left the bar yesterday. I guess this doesn't come as a big surprise," Pauahi said this to herself, as if she were processing my information for the first time.

Was I wrong? Did Kalei just leave by his own volition? His drive to succeed as an actor surpassed whatever connection we had, and whatever connection he claimed to have to the island. Pauahi reached her hand across the bar, searching my eyes for acceptance of her gesture. I fell into the nearest bar stool and placed both of my hands on the bar, leaving them to be felt, cut, burned. I really didn't care. I looked up at the black television screen. In the pale light, I could see it was covered in a thick layer of dust. Pauahi remained standing, her arm still extended toward me, unsure of her next move. I tried to recount the events of the previous day. Kalei left to sign some papers. He was gone long enough for me to become uncomfortable, trying to avoid eye contact with Pauahi. And yet he also left me feeling hopeful and wanted. *I want you all to myself.* How could that same person vanish for the mere opportunity to become a soap star? If his letter were the truth, then he would have gone directly home after we parted. Did he make up his mind on the drive home? Did he start packing right away? When did he write the letter and how did it get to the hotel? He must have come in early, to let his co-workers know and drop the letter off—or maybe he dropped it off somewhere in the middle of the night with special instructions. My mind fluttered, its wings debilitated by the madness of mystery.

"Can I get you anything, Sarah?"

Pauahi's voice softened, her words becoming less clipped and more fluid. She moved her hand further toward me and squeezed the top of my left hand. I had no reaction. My hand didn't flinch, nor did I take any action toward acknowledging the affection.

"Margarita?" Pauahi said with a lilt in her voice, and smiled.

"No, thank you," I said, looking down at her hand on mine. Her skin was much darker than mine, and, while it looked dry, it felt quite smooth.

"I'm sorry," she said before taking her hand back.

"I just don't get it. One day someone wants to be with you, and the next...why did you say it didn't surprise you?"

"Like I said yesterday, he's a boy. This life he made for himself here, I never knew if it was real for him. I questioned that. He's full of energy and talent, and that is very attractive. I can see why you would be drawn to him."

"Do you think I'm a bad woman, a bad wife?"

Pauahi seemed surprised by my question. I took her hesitance to respond as an affirmative and covered my face with my right hand.

"I don't know much about you, Sarah. How could I make such a bold judgment?"

Fair enough, I thought. Despite my initial intentions of blasting Pauahi with blame, I started to feel a modicum of comfort in her presence. I realized I was talking honestly about my situation for the first time with another woman. The quiet of the bar was a welcome change of scenery from the rental car.

"Are you married?" I asked Pauahi.

"I was once," she said, without any follow up.

"Didn't work out?" I pushed and then hoped I hadn't brought up a painful death story.

She turned to look at the clock behind the bar, measuring the time it would take to describe her previous marriage.

"No, I made a mistake. Married very young. The first few years were exciting, filled with passion and clever exchanges. Then, one day, it all stopped. I woke up and saw this strange person who wanted so much of me, demanded even. The more time passed, the more despicable he became to me. He was never violent, or even heartless. In fact, he was a very polite man. We went on eating meals together, talking about the news and other easy matters. Then, one day, he was driving; we had to run some errands on the other side of the island. I kept feeling this urge to open up the passenger door and leap out, hurl myself at the highway, scraping away every inch of my life, so I could start over. I'd be bloodied, but, in time, the scabs would heal and signal a new chapter. Of course, I didn't jump. But when we returned that night, I told him I wouldn't be making dinner and went for a walk. When I returned to find him eating a bowl of canned chili on the living room sofa, I said nothing and continued to our bedroom where I packed up my clothes. I returned to the living room and told him I would be leaving the next morning. We spent one last night together, lying in a bed deplete of feeling. Neither of us ever raised our voice. Sometimes, things just aren't meant to go on too long."

The story had me perked up in my stool, startled by Pauahi's eloquence. Was such a civil divorce really possible? She had not shed a single tear when telling the story, but a discernible movement had taken place within her. Drifting back in time, she connected sharply with the disappointment of her youth.

"Thank you for telling me," I said, almost smiling.

"You'll be okay, Sarah."

"I just feel like such an idiot." I covered my face with both hands.

"You're not an idiot. You're an optimist," Pauahi leaned in as she said it.

My hands fell to the bar, opening my face up. An optimist? I thought about the word, trying to recall a time I had ever met the definition. No one had ever called me this, not that they necessarily called me a pessimist. Just neutral, maybe, or no one really noticed. Optimist. Huh.

"I just don't get it," I went on. "He seemed so into this place, teaching me stuff. He got so upset and protective when a guy tried to sell me a flute at the waterfall, and then he had this whole story about how he changed his name, and then there was the whole proverb about letting the singer sing."

A curious look came over Pauahi's face. She seemed to be remembering something and then calibrating. Finally, she cleared her throat and asked me a question.

"That proverb. Do you remember much about it?"

"I couldn't say it. I mean, I saw it on a piece of paper once, and he said it to me. He just said the meaning had to do with letting a higher power take care of you."

"*Aia no I ka mea e mele ana?*" Pauahi rattled off quickly.

"That's it, I think. I recognize it."

"I told that to him. People always misinterpret the meaning. The true translation is that you are in control of your life. Trust in yourself to decide."

Great, I thought. Once again, I had been played. What was I supposed to think, though? I didn't speak a shred of Hawaiian, and the story was nice. Did it really matter? I thought about the two translations a bit more, and then needed to clear my head of Kalei for as long as my will would allow.

It was getting close to opening time at the bar. Pauahi's body language suggested that she had multiple tasks to accomplish. I fidgeted in my bar stool.

"Hey, Pauahi, have you seen a cat around? Gray, skinny, with a black spot on its head?"

All the color and vitality seemed to drip out of Pauahi's face, leaving her motionless and grim. She covered her face with her left hand, as if she was about to vomit.

"I'm sorry. Is everything okay?" I asked.

"I know that cat. I found him two days ago in a trash can by the employee parking lot."

As difficult as it had been to believe that Kalei had fled overnight across the country, gripping the idea of that cat not being alive was utterly indefinable. I threw an imaginary net into the air in hopes of catching some sort of explanation. I didn't even know if it was a boy or girl cat. It was just there, and now I could never look for it again. I thought of the giant bag of cat food feeling lonely and useless now, wasting away in the backseat of a rental car.

Chapter 14

~

B efore Michael, I would spend just about every Sunday at my parents' house, doing laundry and eating one of my favorite meals. My mother would ask me what I wanted early in the week, so she could plan her shopping. My favorites were her meat lasagna and chicken marsala. Though both were Italian, we had no bloodlines leading back to Italy, nor did I harbor a particular notion toward anything Italian. It just so happened that my mother executed those dishes well. I looked forward to the visits, getting out of my tiny apartment and densely packed neighborhood to breathe fresh air and recharge for the work week.

It was a plain old Sunday like that, two weeks before I met Michael, and my mother was cooking the meat sauce for the lasagna in the kitchen. My father was mowing the back lawn. I seated myself at the kitchen table to watch her, a full glass of red wine in front of me. We exchanged small talk and updated each other on the week's main events. My great-aunt's health was failing. The nursery down the street was going out of business. My parents were considering a cruise to Alaska after hearing what a fantastic experience it was from the neighbors. I had a busy week at work, making great progress on several competing projects. I had tried a spin class, roasted my first chicken, and bought a new skirt.

Sitting back in my chair, I noticed two stacks of books behind me: paperbacks of Sydney Sheldon novels, a book on cake decorating, and a very dated version of *Microsoft Excel for Dummies* comprised one stack. To its right, an array of coffee table books—

likely gifts—lay at the bottom of the heap, topped with a thesaurus, an almanac, and a guide to San Francisco's best restaurants. The cherry on top of this cake of randomness was a small book with an unassuming beige cover. Out of curiosity, I picked it up, thinking I might recognize the title. *The Ladies' Book of Etiquette and Manual of Politeness* by Florence Hartley. I had never seen the book before. I opened up the cover and noted it was originally published in 1872.

"Mom, what's going on with these books?" I asked.

"Oh, I've been going through my shelves. Need to get rid of some stuff," she casually responded, turning away from the stove briefly.

"Are you giving all of these away?"

"Oh, no! The stack on the left is to donate, and the one on the right I'm keeping."

I looked down at the little book of etiquette in my hands, which had come from the stack on the right, and laughed out loud.

"What's so funny?" my mother asked.

I flipped through the pages, betting I would quickly find evidence of hilarity. I touched my fingers down on a page with the header MORNING DRESSES and began to read aloud:

"'The most suitable dress for breakfast is a wrapper made to fit the figure loosely, and the material, excepting when the winter weather requires woolen goods, should be of chintz, gingham, brilliante, or muslin. A lady who has children, or one accustomed to perform for herself light household duties, will soon find the advantage of wearing materials that will wash. A large apron of domestic gingham, which can be taken off if the wearer is called to see unexpected visitors, will protect the front of the dress, and save washing the wrapper too frequently. If a lady's domestic duties require her attention for several hours in the morning, whilst her list of acquaintances is large, and she has frequent morning calls, it is best to dress for callers before breakfast, and wear over this dress a loose sack and skirt of domestic gingham. This, while protecting the dress perfectly, can be taken off at a moment's notice if callers are announced.

Married ladies often wear a cap in the morning, and lately, young girls have adopted the fashion. It is much better to let the hair be perfectly smooth, requiring no cap, which is often worn to conceal the lazy, slovenly arrangement of the hair.'"

My mother finally cut me off, giggling to herself at first, and then turning defensive.

"There are some timeless tips in there if you apply the right filter," she said.

I looked up, scrutinizing her outfit for gingham or chintz. She did wear an apron, but it was a solid white with her initials embroidered across the front in emerald green.

"Mom, how can this be in the keep file? Have you lost your mind? How long have you had this old thing?" I asked, no longer laughing.

"I don't know, Sarah," she snapped at me.

She then went to the refrigerator and pulled out a block of hard cheese. Quickly, she moved to the counter, opened up a cupboard to pull out a cheese grater, and then slammed the cupboard shut. She continued to grate the cheese fastidiously onto a wood cutting board that was already sitting on the counter.

"Sorry, Mom. It's just weird. I mean, don't you think this stuff is kind of, I don't know, dated and sexist and basically, you know, ridiculous?"

I waited for her to turn around, but she just kept on grating the cheese, occasionally adjusting the position of the grater. Fine, I thought. If she wants to hold onto a book of etiquette for whatever reason, that's fine. I flipped through the book without much concentration, registering the page headings every five pages or so. My mother finished her cheese project and finally turned around.

"It's embarrassing. That's all. Can we not talk about it?"

"Sure, I guess."

A loud, grinding sound came from the back of the house, almost shaking me out of my seat. I looked up at my mother who was unfazed, just gliding around the kitchen like a teenager on roller blades.

"Your father must have hit a rock again. I told him he'll break that lawn mower," she said, gliding to the oven to slide in a warming tray with two loaves of bread. Why so much bread for three people? As soon as the oven door shut, an epiphany came over my mother, and she quickly flung open the oven door and removed the bread. Then, with exact precision, she bent down to a low cupboard and pulled out her lasagna pan, opened a package of no-boil lasagna noodles next to the stove, and began layering noodles, sauce, and then cheese with extreme dexterity.

I took a sip of wine and then returned to the book.

Confused by both the appearance of the book and my mother's erratic behavior, I focused back on the pages in front of me. I grazed, thinking I might absorb some nugget of wisdom that would validate one's possession of such oppressive text. I stopped at a section on travel and began reading to myself:

"There is no situation in which a lady is more exposed than when she travels, and there is no position where a dignified, ladylike deportment is more indispensable and more certain to command respect."

Exasperated, I firmly closed the book and set it back on top of my mother's keep pile. I must have let out an audible sigh because my mother shot me a disappointed look before pulling three dinner plates out of a cabinet. I wanted to discuss this more, this strange book attaching itself to my mother. Why wouldn't she talk about it? Was there some significance eluding me? Maybe I should borrow it, I thought. But the mere thought of reading a book like that in its entirety caused my breathing to constrict. I decided to just change the subject.

"Need any help with dinner, Mom?"

"No, just need to let the lasagna bake. Let's go into the living room and relax with our wine."

We moved to the living room, my mother sitting in her favorite leather rocking chair while I spread out on the larger of the two sofas. After twenty minutes or so, my mother returned to the kitchen to make a salad and keep an eye on the lasagna. I would never bring up the book with anyone, especially my father, who would probably not pay much attention if he came across it in the house. As I sat alone in the living room, I looked around at all the personal touches of the room, all the elegant finishes. A dull, sad feeling crept over me. Invading my mother's privacy, possibly causing her shame, had left me alone in my judgment. At no time in my life had I felt more distant from her, and she was just in the other room making one of her typical green salads.

My father and I did most of the talking during dinner, as we hadn't yet had a chance to catch up. My mother remained quiet, but not aloof, occasionally interjecting a comment or question. The dinner was perfect, as always, and there would be plenty of leftovers to get me through the early part of the week.

After dinner, I offered to clear the table, but my mother insisted I relax. I escaped downstairs to check my laundry in the dryer. I had set the timer for too long; my towels were almost too hot to touch. I let them cool a few minutes while I studied the shelves of cleaners, spare light bulbs, and jars once filled with homemade jam now filled with old nails my dad kept around to make him feel like a handyman.

When my laundry was touchable, I scooped it all out into my travel laundry basket, a collapsible mesh tube that reminded me of a slinky. I began taking one item out at a time, setting it on top of the dryer, and folding it. After two towels and a T-shirt, I heard someone coming downstairs. Was it my mother coming to explain the etiquette book in private?

"Finishing up your laundry?"

It was my father, looking pensive with his right hand made into a tight fist. He clearly had something weighing on him.

"Yep, almost done," I said, trying to maintain a light tone.

"How's the apartment?" he asked.

He hated my apartment, a cracker box adjacent to the Tenderloin District with no intercom system or parking garage.

"Same as always." I returned to folding my laundry, unnerved by our stilted conversation. Just minutes ago, we conversed so normally at the dinner table.

"Sarah, I have something I want to talk to you about."

My father took a few steps, shuffles really, toward me and paused. I knew this look, this tone. He wanted to ask if I was dating.

"Are you seeing anyone special?" he asked.

Am I seeing *anyone*? Why even bother with the word *special*?

"You're getting older, you know, and I just worry."

"I'm only twenty-seven, Dad. And this isn't the sixties."

I turned away from him and returned to folding my laundry. *When would he get that I wasn't just like Nancy? Is my life so pathetic in his eyes?*

"I'm sorry, Sarah. I know this is a sensitive thing. A colleague of mine has a daughter close to your age. He was telling me about these websites, you know, where young people can meet each other."

I let a pair of socks fall out of my hands and land on the top of the dryer. It was still warm. Holding back a less civil reaction, I simply turned and said, "I'm familiar with online dating, Dad."

A hint of optimism came over him, helping his body release some of its rigidity.

"Oh, so are you on there then? I mean, do you go to these websites?"

"No, not really my thing. Kind of takes the alive part out of it, don't you think?"

"At first, that's what I thought. But then I heard more about them, and there all sorts of different sites, catering to whichever niche you might fall into."

I laughed a little to myself, picturing my father researching "niche dating sites" and his astonished expression when he sifted through the search results. He finally unclasped his right hand, revealing a small piece of paper. He grasped it between his middle and index fingers and then extended it toward me.

"What's this?" I asked, reaching out and taking the thin paper. Sure enough, it was a website address for a dating site. I looked up at him in despair.

"It's one of these sites, the one my colleague's daughter used. Apparently, they cater to young men with burgeoning careers and strong educations."

My father stared at me, relentlessly hoping for a positive response. I looked down at the web address again, and then flipped the receipt over: milk, flour, golden raisins, toilet paper, can of tomatoes. A part of me wanted to tear it up and shout, decry chauvinism, renounce the need for a husband. Another part of me wanted both my parents to love me, to not worry, to have confidence in my well-being. I tucked the receipt into the bottom of my laundry basket and gave my father a hug.

"Thanks, Dad," I said.

"I love you, Sarah," he said with a shaky voice.

I had no intention of ever visiting that address, but didn't think it hurt for my father to imagine me trolling the Internet for a rich husband. However, the next night, while seated in front of the computer eating leftover lasagna from a plastic container, I started to get curious. I navigated to the site, which had the same format as others I'd visited on similarly curious-but-not-committed occasions. This site would not allow you to view any profiles until you signed up. I thought of my father's face when he handed me the web address, and then my mind darted back to the discomfort I felt with my mother the night before. I clicked on "create a profile" to see what signing up would entail. I started typing in my name and then stopped, taking a few more bites of lasagna. Could I do this? Maybe I was lonely, but this wasn't me at all. But then I thought, What the hell, maybe this will be something to write about some day. I completed my profile in less than twenty minutes and uploaded a picture from Nancy's wedding. After turning the computer off that night, I expected I'd forget about it. It would just become that thing I did once on a lark, and now my information was out there for lurking men in their twenties.

I let two days go by without checking for messages, two long and cruel days. There were no messages. Fine, I thought, this confirms this is not for me. Another five days went by, and I found it easier to ignore the website, such as when one slowly pulls away from a bad habit. Then, exactly one week after I had created the profile, I checked again. There was one message from a guy named Michael Chizeck. *Hi, there. Like your profile. Great pic. Message me if you're interested in grabbing a drink sometime.* I immediately clicked on his profile and tried to absorb and memorize everything about him. *Business school. Likes golf. Loves good wine and travel. Works a lot, but looking for something to help me cut down on that. Seeking balance.* Seeking balance. I liked that. He had four pictures, three of him golfing. He had a cute face and a nice frame, though I did not have any instant sexual attraction through the computer.

Michael and I spent the next several days messaging back and forth, getting to know a little bit more about each other—work, family, favorite foods, least favorite foods, movies, music—basic first date kind of stuff. On the third day of messaging, Michael asked me out to dinner the following weekend. I had no reason to decline, so we agreed to meet at one of his favorite Italian restaurants in North Beach. He was much more attractive in person. His confidence had a soothing effect on me. He took initiative in ordering for us. The meal and conversation were pleasant. On the way out of the restaurant, he kissed me on the cheek and told me he had a really nice time. We agreed to lie about how we met; mutual friends seemed an obvious fabrication. After that night, I started to embrace the new feeling of normalcy in my life. Relaxed by the idea of common conversation with others, I resolved to allow for this person in my future. After our second date, I deleted my online profile and never checked the site again.

Chapter 15

~

A cardinal comes into my peripheral vision, sitting stately on the ledge of the balcony. I turn to stare into its eyes, then beyond to the calm sea. There is something almost eerie about the lack of surf; it's almost like the entire ocean decided to take a nap. For some reason, my mind wanders back to the aftermath of that first date with Michael, that sense of nascent belonging to a world that one could never escape. The cardinal remains in the same spot as I hear the key card slide into the door.

It's time. I sit up straight in the chair, looking once more at the cardinal, and then into the mirror out of habit, one last check before the event. As Michael enters, I know immediately he hasn't been golfing. His eyes are bloodshot, his entire being drained of its life force. He speaks first, standing in front of the door.

"Let me go first. I've been thinking all day about this, about us."

Michael moves to the sofa and sits exactly where he'd sat earlier that morning. He clasps his hands and looks down at them as if they were foreign appendages.

"Did you notice a fern when you went to the volcano? There's a fern that grows out of the lava there. I think it's called *kupukupu* or something like that. There was this video in the gift shop about all the plants that grow in the park, and this fern is known for its resiliency. I mean, it basically thrives out of barren nothingness. To survive in that kind of challenging environment, it's amazing. Sarah, I think we're like that, you know. We'll get through whatever is in front of us, and thrive. We're

Michael and Sarah. So, I guess, after spending the day thinking and thinking, I came to the conclusion that it doesn't matter what's going on with you. I don't need to know. We're going to be just fine, just like that fern. I know we aren't perfect, but that's okay. We figure out what works and whatever that is *has* to be better than being alone. I love you. We have to work. There's no alternative."

To say I am caught off guard would be a colossal understatement. I look away from him, focus on the cardinal, and imagine hundreds of them, covering every surface with brilliant red feathers. The image brings a smile to my face, confusing Michael, perhaps bringing a false hope. My gaze returns to him, and he looks relieved. But the relief sours to concern after a twitchy silence bounces between us. Finally, Michael stands up to address me, still seated in front of the mirror.

"Are you going to say anything?" he asks with his face aghast.

How do I respond? My mind races back to my journal, my ridiculous list of pros and cons. My epic choice of two great men. I want to acknowledge Michael's effort.

"That was very thoughtful, Michael. Thank you."

He touches my shoulders, trying to sink back into my heart by way of cutting through my extreme tension. Relief resurfaces in his eyes and lips. A part of me wants him to keep touching me.

"And? So we're good?" he asks, resting his hands on the sides of my neck.

Looking at him, seeing his image behind me through the mirror, I begin to see him in the park after a long run. I see him trying to tell me he loves me with his toothbrush hanging from his mouth. I see him fidget standing in line to buy peanut butter. I watch these flashes—a slideshow someone sends out after a vacation. My vacation marriage. I grip the outer edges of the desk, asking myself one last time if I'm ready.

"No, we're not. I'm not," I say with a heavy exhale of relief.

Michael removes his hands from my neck, turns away from me, and then paces behind me, coming in out of view in the mirror. He speaks in a frenetic, bargaining, desperate tone. I'd never seen this part of him.

"I told you we don't need to talk about it. I get that you're not always happy with me, with us. Like I said, we'll work through it. I'll work harder."

He stops pacing and begins wringing his hands, touching his wedding ring: a simple gold band we picked out together one foggy morning at a small jeweler on Market Street. This wasn't the plan, my plan. I strain to stay calm, to avoid matching his heightened tone, but my words end up choppy and vague.

"I wasn't expecting to...I expected to speak first, so I'm a little flustered here."

Michael turns around, gripping opposite elbows.

"Don't speak!" he yells at me. He never yells. I feel my pulse pick up speed, and the skin on my cheeks sizzles like the exposed shoulders of the young women sunning by the pool. Only there is absolutely no sunlight in this room. I feel confused by his rage before realizing its appropriateness.

"What?" I ask without a hint of defensiveness.

"I mean, that's not what I mean. You know what I mean," he stammers.

In no mood to read his mind, a surge of frustration shoots up from my gut.

"I don't know. But I know what I want," I blurt out in release.

Michael turns to look at me through the mirror again with a searching look in his eyes. I realize that he has no idea what I am about to say.

"What?" he asks with his mouth and eyes.

This is where I knew I had options. I could remain calm and collected, coming across like an ice queen. Or I could give in to it all, admit my hesitation right up until this moment; I could cry and let Michael hug me. I would keep saying "I don't know anymore" and then move to the veranda where I would take the deepest and most important gaze of my life. But I pick the first option, hoping to infuse some hint of consideration where I could. It was the only way I could achieve what I lusted after more than anything in the world.

"I've packed up my stuff in the other room. I'm not flying back to San Francisco with you."

"You're joking, right?" Michael says as he leans into me. His breath smells like a Band-Aid. I move my face away from him, staying seated in the chair. I look toward the front door of the room and try to remember the room number. Is it 1149?

"I'm sorry," I say. "We can work out the logistics later. I'll send for some of my things, and you can do what you want with the rest."

There is an apology to be made, but I risk too much in the moment to convey one. Michael smashes his hand down onto the desk, causing it to shake. He then springs away from it, away from me and begins pacing again.

"Wait! You're staying *here*?" he screams. "You hate the tropics! You didn't even want to come here!"

"You brought me here." And, indeed, he did. Against all my subtle protestations.

Michael laughs, mockingly, covering his face with his hands. He walks toward the sliding door to the veranda, but there is no penetrating gaze out to the sea. He just peers down to look at his shoes.

"How will you survive?" he asks, emphasizing *survive*. How on earth would someone like me pay rent? I already have that covered.

"I'm staying with my friend Pauahi for a while until I can find work."

Michael looks toward the bedroom door, which is closed. I wonder if he's thinking about the sex we had in there—the orgasms he gave himself credit for the time I fantasized about Kalei. Michael and I would never see each other naked again. I might miss that.

"Who's this friend? How did you make a friend in less than two weeks?" he asks, still staring at the bedroom door.

"She works in one of the lounges here. I spent a lot of time drinking." I could go for one of her margaritas right now. Or sixteen. Michael looks away from the bedroom door, his eyes darting around the room before landing on me as he began his appeal.

"You can't survive here, Sarah. You know that. Don't you think you're being selfish? After everything I've—"

"Stop! I knew you would do this," I cut him off, not wanting to hear about my supposed inability to support myself.

"Do what? Do what?" Michael asks, returning to his incredulous laughter.

I need to economize the conversation, to put the final deadbolt on our marriage, so we can just stop talking. I start in my most transactional tone.

"I don't want any money. I know this sounds crazy to you, but it makes total sense to me. It's absolutely decided. My wedding ring is on your bedside table."

Michael's entire being deflates; I feel his energy draining into the floor under my feet. He is small, fatigued, and utterly gray. He moves to the sofa and collapses into the fetal position, clutching a pillow to his heart. He bites his lip, holds back the tears, and gently rocks back and forth.

"Am I bad in bed? Do I not spend enough time at home? Is it my family? Your family? I just don't understand!"

I give Michael my most appreciative stare through the mirror, but he isn't making eye contact. He's managed to hold back the tears and is no longer rocking.

"I don't expect you to. Ever. Just take care of yourself, Michael. This is my mess, not yours." These are my last words to the man I let become my husband.

A quiet storm of emotion overwhelms Michael, suppressing his ability to speak. He stands up, rushes to the door, and then turns to look at me. Had it been the face of hatred, animosity, disappointment—anything else—that final moment would have been less painful. But that last look I get from Michael is a profound blankness. I attempt a smile with my eyebrows, but it was too late. Michael vanishes from the room. I look at myself again in the mirror and consider my own looks. Is that a pretty face? What would become of it after years in the hot sun? My own doubts that swished around in the moments before Michael's entrance evaporate along with Michael. My head and chest are light like a balloon, but my gut is heavy. I want to vomit, but somehow I know the feeling will pass.

And I never will tell Michael about Kalei. I will never tell anyone other than Pauahi. It will just live inside me, that thing that happened once upon a time when I didn't know how to speak.

Chapter 16

~

Pauahi was not exaggerating when she said that this beach was a challenge to locate. I drive down a bumpy dirt road in her truck that she's let me borrow. "This is the best spot for a morning swim," she said. I drive by each light pole slowly, staring to discern the number. I finally hit Pole 67, the unofficial name of this hideaway local beach. I park the truck and begin my hike. After several feet, I rise to a bluff that overlooks the most pristine water I've ever seen—glassy, calm, ethereal. Delighted and nervous, I make my way down to the beach. It's just before eight o'clock. I only see one person in the water. I pause for a moment to see something moving in a banyan tree: an orange cat chasing after a bird. I smile as I wind down to the bottom of the trail and hit my feet to the sand. The person in the water is a woman. She's swimming to shore. Now she's standing up. She's familiar. It's Angela, the bartender.

"Good morning," Angela says as she wrings out her hair and wipes the salt water from her eyes.

I wonder if she remembers me. Should I introduce myself?

"How's the water?" I ask.

"Perfect. Hey, do we know each other?" she asks.

She remembers me!

"Yes. I was staying at the hotel. I came in a few times to get drinks."

"Oh, right. I made you one of my fruity concoctions. I'm Angela," she reaches out her hand.

"Hi, I'm Sarah," I say as my dry hand grasps her slippery one.

"How'd you end up down here? Kind of an obscure spot?" Angela asks.

"I actually live here now," I say, aloud, for the first time.

"Welcome to the island. You're kama`aina now," she says.

My heart begins to pound. I must seize this opportunity. She can help me do what I need to do this morning.

"This might sound weird, but could I ask you a favor?"

"Sure," she responds with a slight question mark.

"I'm not a very good swimmer. In fact, I've always been afraid of the water, especially the ocean. There was this girl in my elementary school who drowned. It was kind of a big deal. It was the summer I started swimming lessons. I only made it through two lessons before my parents made me quit. 'Too risky,' they said. They couldn't think of a reason for me to ever have a need to swim. When I protested, my father sat me down and told me in detail what happens to the human body when it drowns. How the throat spasms and relaxes. How osmosis pulls water from the bloodstream into the lungs, thickening the blood. I guess you could say it was very effective. It's funny, though. I always just told people it was a deep but generic phobia. Anyway, would you stay here while I swim out? When I wave, then you'll know that it's okay to leave. I could use that little safety net."

Angela is wearing a black bikini top and a pair of tight purple men's swim trunks. She smiles and reaches her arm out to pat me on the shoulder.

"Of course," she says.

"Thanks," I say. I remove my shorts, T-shirt, and sandals and make my way to the water before another question comes to me that I must ask Angela. I turn around and raise my voice above the slow movement of the water. "Would it be okay if I come in to the bar sometime? Since I'm new, I don't really have many friends."

"Please do," Angela says.

I turn around, smiling, and wade out into the water. Inch by inch, I become more submerged. I stop when the water reaches above my waist. *Go under. It's time.* A giant breath—the longest breath of my life—precedes the buckling of my knees. Chin touches the water. Eyes close. My legs become springs, surging me forward and under. *Keep going.* I come up for air, my arms and legs wiggling below the water. I look to the shore and spot Angela, jumping up and down and waving both arms. I worry what waving will do to me. Will I sink? My treading increases in my legs as I raise one hand. I give a thumbs-up. Angela responds with two thumbs-ups and waves some more. She's making sure I'm stable. I wave again, signaling for her departure. It's time to be alone here. I watch as she ascends the cliff and then fades into the young morning air.

Assured, I relax into a steady pace, treading in the warmth of the morning sea. I close my eyes, feeling the luxury of the water against my body. The heat that Kalei ignited in me is still there, never to swim away. I open my eyes and rotate in circles to soak up every living moment in my own private ecosystem. A wave of subtle satisfaction rubs against me. I look to the shore, which seems odd and distant. I look out to the open sea, in the opposite direction of San Francisco. I swim a little further away. And a little further. *I'm not drowning.* Here, in this greatly untethered place, I surrender to my own arrival.

Acknowledgments

~

I would like to briefly thank just a few of the many people who made writing and publishing this book a possibility. First and foremost I give my deepest gratitude to Dan Garlington and Ruth Haney for being my early fans. Your support as well as critique kept the project alive. Thank you to my generous and supportive family, especially my mother, for taking a keen interest in the work. Jennifer Hager, thank you for your magic touch in refining my manuscript and for being a cheerleader. To the fine folks at Hugo House, I appreciate very much the resources and feedback. Finally, I'd like to give my warmest aloha to all the beautiful people who reside on the Big Island and who have helped shape and inspire this story. Aloha mau loa!

About the Author

⟡

Dan Dembiczak is a Seattle native who began writing stories as soon as he could spell. He earned a BA in creative writing from the University of Washington, and has worked extensively in local theater as a playwright, actor, director, and producer. Eight of his plays were produced in Seattle, including the popular four-part Capitol Hill High series, and a number of his articles and short stories have appeared in publications in Seattle and Los Angeles.

Dembiczak has traveled extensively to the Hawaiian islands, particularly the Big Island, where he was married in 2008, and considers Hawai'i his second home. He primarily resides in Seattle with his husband, dog, and chickens, and is currently working on his second novel, *The Hardest Pose is Corpse Pose*, which tells the tale of a yoga teacher facing change, adultery, and, possibly, death.

Made in the USA
Charleston, SC
18 March 2014